DR DELISLE'S INHERITANCE

Perhaps Community Midwife Abigail Brent should have guessed before her marriage to popular Dr Marcus DeLisle that he had an ulterior motive in proposing to her. But by the time she finds out it is too late, and Abigail has no alternative but to work with her new husband in his Guernsey practice . . .

DR DELISLE'S INHERITANCE

BY

SARAH FRANKLIN

MILLS & BOON LIMITED
15–16 BROOK'S MEWS
LONDON W1A 1DR

CHAPTER ONE

'WHAT'S YOUR name, Nurse—your Christian name, I mean?' Mrs Jeffreys was drowsy with pethidine. She had been in the first stage of labour for ten hours now and her forehead was beaded with perspiration.

Abigail gently wiped it with a damp flannel. 'Abigail, believe it or not,' she said, glad that her patient was now able to think of something else besides the pain. 'My mother was determined to give me an original name. Most people call me Abby, but that's not much better, is it?'

'I think it's pretty—different as you say. I've been trying to think of unusual names for the baby—' She stopped speaking as another contraction gripped her and Abigail patted her hand.

'Try to relax, Mrs Jeffreys. Remember your deep breathing. The injection helps quite a lot, doesn't it?'

'Yes, it does.' Janet Jeffreys sighed. 'Oh dear. I shouldn't really be having this baby at all—not at my age.' The eyes that looked up at Abigail were dark with apprehension. 'John and I always knew it was chancy but we wanted a baby so much. Dr DeLisle was so kind. He explained everything to us. He was perfectly frank about the risks. It all seemed well worth it at the time—now I'm not so sure.'

Abigail wiped the damp brow again, shaking her head. She could see the tell-tale signs that her patient was moving towards the second stage. The confinement was going very well, considering that her patient was well past the usual age for a first baby.

'I think it's a little too late to change your mind now,' she said with a smile. 'Don't worry. You're doing marvellously and Dr DeLisle will be here soon, getting ready to deliver your baby. It won't be long now. Why don't you try to get some rest until the injection wears off? If you need me you have only to ring the bell.'

Janet Jeffreys nodded drowsily as the contraction released her from its grip. 'I'll be all right. I expect you think I'm silly. It's just—just—' Her eyes closed and Abigail tiptoed out of the small side ward, dimming the lights as she went towards the office to bring her report up to date. Janet Jeffreys was forty-three and hadn't the stamina of a younger woman. She was very tired indeed. This was one confinement that Abigail would be relieved to have behind her.

As she went into the office Joan Marshall, the night sister, looked up from her desk. 'How is she?'

'Tired,' Abigail said briefly. 'But so far everything is going normally. I think I'll ring Dr DeLisle and get him to come in. I've a feeling things will start moving before long.' She picked up the receiver and dialled the number.

'Didn't the husband come in with her?' Joan asked.

Abigail shook her head. 'He took one sniff when we arrived and turned bright green! Anyway, they'd already decided that they didn't want him to be present at the birth. I packed him off home and told him I'd ring him as soon as there was any news.'

Joan smiled. 'Very diplomatic. We can do without a swooning daddy!'

The telephone had rung several times before a sleepy voice answered, 'Hello—Dr DeLisle here.'

'Nurse Brent—it's Mrs Jeffreys, Doctor. Everything is normal—going well so far. She's moving towards the second stage.'

'Right. I'm on my way.' He sounded fully alert now. 'See you in about ten minutes, Abby.'

Her heart lifted at the use of her first name. It was almost four weeks now since Marc DeLisle had last taken her out, and she had been trying hard to face the fact that their brief affair was probably over—trying to convince herself that she was only infatuated with him and not really in love. After all, the charm of Dr Marcus DeLisle was well known in the GP Unit of the Wellbourne Maternity Hospital. He was by far the most popular doctor among nursing staff and patients too, with his good looks and attractive personality.

As she replaced the receiver on its rest, Joan Marshall looked up at her, taking in the tell-tale expression on Abigail's face and the way her teeth caught at her lower lip.

'Tell me to mind my own business if you like, but I thought you and he had a thing going.'

'So did I for a while,' Abigail confessed. Joan had been her friend ever since she had completed her training and come to work as a community midwife in the small East Midlands town of Rinkley. 'I went overboard for that charm of his and read more into it than I should have done, I suppose. Anyway, I haven't been out with him for weeks, so I suppose that's that.'

Joan looked at her sympathetically. 'Do you mind very much?'

Abigail shrugged in an attempt at indifference. 'Not really.'

'Just as well considering he's leaving soon.' Joan returned her attention to the work in front of her, unaware of the impact of her casual remark. Abigail cleared her throat.

'Leaving? I hadn't heard—are you sure?' Her heart plummetted. Even though she was trying hard to get over the disappointment that Marc hadn't asked her out again, she hadn't entirely given up hope. He lived a very busy life as a partner in a local group practice—free time was at a premium, she knew that all too well. But if he was *leaving* . . . She stared at Joan's back, moistening her lips and hoping her voice wouldn't give her away as she asked, 'Why is he going? It's all very sudden, isn't it?'

Joan turned to look at her. 'Well, I only know what I've heard on the grapevine, of course, but it seems—' Her words were interrupted by a sudden sharp buzzing and Abigail started up.

'That's Mrs Jeffreys. I had a feeling things would start moving soon.' She looked at her watch. 'I hope Marc—Dr DeLisle—gets here soon.'

Joan stood up. 'I'll alert the delivery room. Good luck, Abby.'

Abigail found that she had been right. A brief examination told her that the time had come to remove her patient to the delivery room. With the aid of a second-year nurse she helped Mrs Jeffreys on to the trolley and they made the short journey down the corridor. As they were transferring her on to the delivery couch she looked up at Abigail nervously.

'I wish John were here.'

Abigail smiled reassuringly. 'Everything is just fine, Mrs Jeffreys. Doctor will be here at any minute. Would you like me to get someone to ring your husband and ask him to come?'

'No—no—he'd only worry—think something was

wrong.' She bit her lip as another pain assailed her and Abigail took one of the tightly clenched hands in hers and leaned over her patient.

'Now, this is where you can work with us, Mrs Jeffreys,' she said. 'Do you remember what you learned at the classes? So far you haven't had much control over what was happening, but now you can help yourself—and us quite a lot. There's help for you too.' She pressed the gas and air mask into the hand she held. 'Breathe it when you feel you need to.' She hadn't heard Marc come into the room and was surprised when she looked up and found his golden-brown eyes smiling at her over his mask. Gloved hands held before him, he smiled down at Mrs Jeffreys.

'Just going to make a little examination now.' he said, his voice slightly muffled by the mask. 'We'll have your baby here in no time—exciting, isn't it?'

She smiled back at him, relaxing visibly. It was amazing what Marcus DeLisle did for his patients, Abigail told herself admiringly. It seemed they had only to see him to feel better. Under the circumstances, Mrs Jeffreys could have been delivered by a consultant obstetrician, but she had chosen to stick with Marc, her own GP, in whom she had every confidence.

The hours that followed were hard work for all three of them. Janet Jeffreys was a cooperative and brave patient, but she was tired and needed all the encouragement they could give her. Dawn was just breaking when Marc leant over her, his eyes gentle and persuasive.

'Just once more, Janet. One more big effort and you'll be holding your baby. Sister Marshall tells me that your husband is in the waiting room. Come along now. You can do it. I know you can.'

Abigail was watching him—admiring his calmness.

She knew that he was growing concerned about the length of the second stage—afraid that the baby would be under stress too long, but he showed no trace of his fears to his patient as he gently encouraged her. Janet managed a weak smile and seemed to rally the last of her strength for him, and a few minutes later the baby was born.

Marc's eyes met Abigail and she saw the relief in them. The child was perfect, the tiny face puckered as it emitted a furious yell. He nodded to her in a gesture that told her that the pleasure of breaking the news to the patient was hers.

'You have a beautiful little daughter, Mrs Jeffreys,' she said, the familiar surge of joy tightening her throat.

'And no need for stitches. Isn't that great?' Marc said. 'I think you're a very clever lady. Miss Jeffreys here seems pretty disgusted with the world at the moment though!'

A relieved laugh rippled round the delivery room and Janet's face was radiant as she looked down at her baby for the first time. 'A little girl—how wonderful. I'm going to call her Abigail.'

Once the third stage was safely over, Marc peeled off his gloves and pulled down his mask to smile at Abigail. 'I'll go and tell the father—that is if he's still in the land of the living! He looked distinctly queasy last time I spoke to him,' he told her quietly. 'Have you any more cases tonight?'

She shook her head. 'This morning, you mean! No, thank goodness. My four days off start after today too. I'm ready for it!'

He paused at the door. 'I'll wait for you,' he said. 'Perhaps we can have a coffee together and unwind.'

Abigail found herself blushing. 'Fine—I'll see you later.'

Marc waved to his patient. 'I'll see you later, Janet. Mind you behave yourself and have a good sleep.'

'I'm far too excited for sleep, Doctor.' Janet's eyes shone. 'Thank you so much—for everything.'

As Abigail came out of the hospital a quarter of an hour later she saw that he was waiting for her in his car, the window wound down. He glanced up at a sky streaked with pearly gold.

'It's going to be another fine day. Maybe we'd better make that breakfast. Shall we go round the corner to the Baytree?'

Abigail climbed gratefully into the passenger seat beside him and drew a long breath. 'That sounds marvellous. The way I feel at this moment I'd fall straight into bed if I went home now.'

'Me too.' He switched on the ignition.

The Baytree was only a few hundred yards from the hospital gates and kept open twenty-four hours a day, which made it a popular place with both staff and visitors. As they sat opposite each other, stirring large cups of coffee and waiting for their bacon and eggs to arrive, Abigail smiled at him.

'I'm so relieved that Mrs Jeffreys has had her baby without complications. She's the oldest first-time mother I've had so far. They wanted that baby so badly. I was terrified in case something should go wrong.'

Marc nodded. 'I'm relieved too. I'll admit it now, though we did all the tests we could to ensure that everything was normal. Regular scanning helped too, of course.' He laughed. 'In the end it was a piece of cake really—a pity she hadn't spent all her life having babies instead of running a business!'

'What a chauvinistic remark!' Abigail retorted. 'As it happens, she enjoyed her career—she told me she didn't start feeling maternal until it was almost too late.'

He shook his head. 'Chauvinistic or not, some women want to have their cake and eat it!' He touched her hand as she opened her mouth to rise to his remark again. 'But I don't want to have an argument with you about sexual equality at this time of the morning, Abby. As a matter of fact, I've got something to tell you.'

His hand felt good on hers, warm and strong, but she gently pulled her own from beneath it, lowering her eyes.

'I think I know what it is. You're leaving, aren't you?'

He looked surprised. 'How did you know?'

She shrugged. 'You know what hospitals are—news travels fast, especially bad news.'

'I see—so you know the reason too?'

She looked up. 'No.'

He looked puzzled. 'You hadn't heard that my father had died then?'

She flushed. 'No! Oh, Marc, I'm so sorry.'

He sighed. 'Yes. It was very sudden. I managed to fly home for the funeral. I believe I told you that he was a doctor too—in Guernsey, my home. He was the senior partner in the family practice, with my uncle and cousin and so, of course, they need me now. My cousin is only with the practice temporarily, you see, so I feel I should go home as soon as I can. There's so much to do.'

'Yes, of course, I see.' Abigail bit her lip, afraid to meet his eye in case he should see the desolation she felt.

'I didn't want to let Bill Curtis down,' Marc went on, referring to the senior partner in the Rinkley practice. 'He and his wife Helen have been so good to me—letting me have the flat at the top of their house and everything.

But Bill says he'll manage with a locum—and of course the easier time of year is coming along, if there is such a thing.' He broke off with a lift of his eyebrows. 'Wait—if you didn't know about my father, why did you say it was *bad* news?'

Her colour deepened. 'I—just meant your going. You'll be missed—by everyone. Don't you know that you're a very popular doctor?'

He smiled and covered her hand with his again. 'I have to admit that it's nice to hear you say so. And what about you—will *you* miss me?'

She looked up at him, trying to brazen out his challenge. 'I dare say I'll manage to struggle on somehow!'

He laughed delightedly and she joined in. Surprisingly it wasn't hard. Marc could always make her laugh. It was one of the nicest things about him, though she had often wished that their relationship could have been more serious. Suddenly the hand that covered hers tightened.

'Abby—have dinner with me tomorrow night.' He shook his head. 'No, I mean tonight, don't I? Midnight deliveries always give me jet-lag. Will you come?'

She looked into the golden eyes, longing to say yes, yet knowing that seeing him, being with him again, would only make his going more painful for her. His eyes searched hers and for the hundredth time she told herself that they were exactly the colour of sherry—and just about as potent.

'Does it take that much thinking about?' he asked teasingly. 'Is it that you have another date or have you just plain old gone off me?'

She swallowed hard. If she didn't go she would spend the rest of her life regretting it; if she did, the whole painful yearning would start up all over again, this time without hope. Had he any idea at all of the chaos he was capable of creating? she wondered resentfully. She would *have* to turn him down!

'Well—what's the answer?'

She glanced up to find him looking at her with that heart-stopping smile. 'Thanks, Marc—that would be very nice,' she heard herself saying weakly.

With a good breakfast inside her she felt better and declined his offer to drive her back to the hospital car park to get her own car. The fresh air would do her good, she told him; help to freshen her up for the drive back to Weston Rise.

She drove home carefully. Weston Rise was the huge sprawling council development where she had her small house. The birds were up now and the sun was shining brightly as she made her way along the snaking by-pass. Once inside, she closed the front door with a sigh and took off her shoes and hat, flexing her toes luxuriously. There would just be time for a bath and a couple of hours' sleep before she made her routine calls. Thank goodness she was due for some time off! She went upstairs and ran the bath, slipping into the bedroom while she waited for it to fill, running the answering machine to see if there were any messages. For once there was nothing urgent—just a call from her mother. She sat on the bed, listening to the slightly petulant voice.

'Oh dear—why is it you're always out when I call? I feel so foolish, talking to my own daughter on an answering machine! Ring me as soon as you can, will you, darling?'

Jennifer Brent had never got used to the fact that her daughter was a midwife. She seemed to find it impossible to take her career seriously. Abigail supposed it came of their seeing each other so infrequently while she was growing up. She wondered if other offspring of divorced parents had the same problems. Jennifer would have to wait for her call now. She certainly wouldn't appreciate being telephoned at five a.m.

Lying in the scented water, Abigail relaxed and thought of Marc. She supposed that the dinner date was intended as a final goodbye. Anyone as popular as he was must have made hordes of friends, both male and female, during his time at Rinkley. How could she have been stupid enough to have allowed herself to fall in love with him? she asked herself crossly. Marc was charming to everyone; she was flattering herself if she thought his attention to her meant anything special. Why couldn't she have been strong enough to have said no when he asked her to have dinner with him? No doubt he would have been grateful for the extra time her refusal would have given him. There must be a lot of people he had to see before he left.

By the time she crept under the duvet, Abigail was feeling depressed and thoroughly annoyed with herself. Perhaps when she woke she would ring Marc and cancel their date. But when the alarm clock jangled mercilessly in her ear two hours later, nothing was further from her mind.

After the routine house-calls, Abigail just had time to drop in at the hospital to see Janet Jeffreys. She found her sitting up in bed, happily chatting to the three other mothers in the ward, while her tiny daughter slept peacefully in a crib beside her.

'I feel an awful fraud,' she whispered to Abigail. 'All these young girls keep asking me for advice. They think that at my age this must be at least my *sixth* baby! So far I haven't had the nerve to tell them it's my first time in here too.'

Abigail laughed. 'Why worry about that? You've had a successful career and now you've had a baby too, so you still have the edge over them. Now, tell me, what does your husband think of his new daughter?'

Janet smiled. 'He's thrilled. I wish you could have seen his face. I can't wait to get home.'

Abigail shook her head. 'I rather think that Dr DeLisle will insist on your staying in for seven days at least,' she warned. 'You need the rest. I'm about to go off for my break, but I'll be in to see you when I come back. There'll be an awful lot to do when you get home, you know,' she added when she saw Janet's disappointed expression. 'You'll need all your strength.'

'It's all going to be such fun!' Janet leaned forward, lowering her voice. 'I've heard a rumour that Dr DeLisle is leaving. It isn't true, is it?'

Abigail nodded. 'I'm afraid so. His father has died, so he has to go home to Guernsey to take over the family practice.'

Janet sighed. 'What a pity. John and I have such faith in him. I hate the idea of having to get used to another doctor now.'

Abigail smiled. 'Dr Curtis is very nice. I'm sure you'll be happy with him. Dr DeLisle will certainly be missed.' As she walked down the corridor a few moments later, she reflected wryly that Marc's absence would leave a gap in the lives of a good many people.

It wasn't until she got home from the ante-natal clinic that afternoon that she remembered her mother's request for her to ring. She glanced at her watch. It was almost five o'clock. Should she ring her now at her office, or should she hang on until she'd had time to get home? She decided to ring now and chance it. If she left it until later and Jennifer wanted to chat, she would have to get ready for her date with Marc in a rush—and she wanted to have plenty of time for that.

Jennifer had been on the point of leaving the building. Her secretary had only just caught her, and when she came to the telephone she sounded breathless and a little put out.

'Darling, you really are the limit! You leave it all day and then ring just as I'm rushing off. I want to catch the shops before they close. There isn't a thing in the flat and I've invited people for supper.'

'Sorry, but I'm going out too, so I won't keep you. I rang because I thought it might be important.' Why was it that she always seemed to be the one apologising?

'I only thought we might have a day together when you next have some time off,' Jennifer said. 'It seems ages since I've seen you. I'm on holiday all next week. How about coming up for the day?'

'Can we make it Monday?' Abigail asked. 'I'm off for the next four days as it happens. Monday will be the only day of next week I can manage.'

'Fine. I'll expect you at the flat at about ten, shall I? Must dash now, darling—bye!' And before Abigail could echo her farewell, her mother had rung off. She hung up thoughtfully. What had Jennifer got up her sleeve this time? This kind of casual invitation usually meant she had news of some kind. Oh well, she would just have to wait and see.

She took a long time getting ready, looking at herself critically in the mirror and wondering which dress suited her best—which hairstyle to choose? She tried it swept up, looking at herself from all angles. It certainly flattered the smooth line of her throat and neck and emphasised her regular features. If only it were a more interesting colour. Jennifer had tried to persuade her to have it lightened, but somehow she had never fancied the idea. She picked up a strand and peered at it glumly. Pale mouse—that was the only way to describe it. After a good dose of sun it streaked quite attractively, but it was too early in the year for that.

She put on a plain black dress and took it off again; it made her look sallow and nondescript. She tried on the red dress she had splashed out on for the party Jennifer had thrown when she had landed her present job, and then she rejected that too, afraid that it might look too frivolous. At last she chose a wine-coloured velvet suit with a white blouse and wore her freshly shampooed hair loose and straight. At least it was abundant and shiny, she told herself as she brushed it smooth. She was only just ready when she heard the doorbell ring. She leapt up from the dressing-table, pausing to count ten at the top of the stairs, afraid that he would think her too eager.

He smiled when she opened the door and, to her surprise, handed her a bunch of red roses. She blushed with pleasure as she took them from him.

'Are they really for me? But why?'

He raised an eyebrow. 'Never question a man's reason for giving you flowers!' He smiled as he stepped inside. 'You did an excellent job last night—how about that? Or what about—I was passing the florist's and they reminded me of you?'

She laughed. 'I'll put them in water right away.'

Marc stood in the kitchen doorway as she searched the cupboard for a vase worthy of such a bouquet. At last she found one and filled it at the tap, acutely aware of his eyes on her as she thrust the long stems into the water. 'There, I'll arrange them properly later.' She turned to him. 'You won't want to wait while I fiddle with them now.'

'I'm not in a hurry,' he said lazily. 'There's no prettier sight than watching a woman arranging flowers, and it's nice to see you doing something you're not very good at for a change. When you're working you're all efficiency.'

Abigail raised an eyebrow. 'Surely that's the way I should be?'

He nodded. 'Of course. I like seeing this side of you too though.' He reached out and grasped her shoulders, drawing her to him, his eyes sweeping appreciatively over her. 'You're looking very lovely tonight. Is all this for me? I feel honoured.'

'I don't actually live in my uniform,' she told him huskily. When she was as close to him as this, something seemed to happen to her breathing. Her heart was bumping unevenly too, making her feel slightly dizzy.

'I'm delighted to hear it.' He bent to kiss her briefly, then looked at her for a long moment. 'It seems ages since we last went out together, Abby. I'm sure you understand though.'

Privately she thought he might have rung her to explain, but she simply nodded. 'Of course—shall we go?'

He smiled, lifting his shoulders slightly. 'If you like. Are you hungry?'

She coloured slightly at the twinkle in his eyes. 'Oh dear, did it sound like that?' She raised her chin to look at him defiantly. 'Anyway, now that you mention it— yes, I am hungry. I've only had time to snatch a sandwich since that enormous breakfast you bought me this morning!'

He took her arm. 'In that case I'd better feed you before you expire completely!'

Sitting beside him in the car, she examined his profile as he concentrated on the traffic. She supposed it must be what was known as 'classical', with the high forehead and strong bones. His hair, like his eyes, was a rich golden brown and curled softly into the nape of his neck. She bit her lip hard and looked away. If only he weren't so attractive—so nice. That charm of his, it wasn't the superficial, 'switched-on' kind. That was why everyone liked him so much. He managed to make each and every one of his patients feel that they were the most interesting and important person he knew—she had heard it from their own lips time and again. Did the same thing apply to his girlfriends? she asked herself, her eyes firmly on the road ahead.

'Abby? You're miles away. I thought you were hungry.'

She started as he spoke, noticing that they had stopped. He had parked the car in the forecourt of the town's smartest and most expensive hotel. He looked at his watch.

'I booked a table for eight o'clock. It's ten to. We've just got time for a drink if you fancy one. Shall we go?'

'Oh, yes—of course.'

In the small bar just off the restaurant he ordered the drinks, then looked at her speculatively. 'Is anything wrong, Abby? You seem a little tense this evening.'

She shrugged. For one hysterical moment she wondered what would happen if she were to tell him the truth—that losing him meant more than he would ever guess. She imagined the look of horrified shock that would cloud his face and swallowed hard, examining her nails. 'I—had a telephone call from my mother earlier today,' she said, clutching at the only straw she could think of. 'She wants me to go up to London on Monday and spend the day with her.'

He laughed gently and pushed her glass towards her. 'Really? Is that so worrying?'

She took a sip of the cocktail he had ordered, grateful for its astringent coolness as it slipped down her throat. 'You don't know my mother. That usually means that she has some sort of bombshell to drop.'

He nodded understandingly. 'She's a career woman, isn't she? I seem to remember you telling me she was a journalist or something like that.'

Abigail nodded. 'She's editor of a magazine called *Julie*. It's aimed at the modern teenager—fashion, careers, the pop scene, that sort of thing. As you know, my father was a doctor. I spent most of my childhood with him because Jennifer was a newspaper reporter in those days and used to be away for a lot of the time. Then, when they were divorced, it seemed easier all round for things to remain as they were.'

'How long is it since your father died?' Marc asked gently.

'Four years.' She looked up at him. 'It's only during that time that Jennifer and I have really got to know one another.' She sighed. 'I understand how you feel about your father, Marc, believe me.'

He lifted his shoulders lightly. 'I imagine it was much worse for you. My father and I were never close. I hardly saw him when I was a child. My mother died when I was very young and I was packed off to boarding school at a very early age. In the holidays I was looked after by a series of rather grudging housekeepers—it wasn't much to look forward to.'

There was a hint of bitterness in his voice and Abigail looked thoughtfully at him. Had he developed that charm of his as a sort of defence—a sure way into people's good books? She thought of the lonely little boy he must have been and her heart twisted. She was about to say something when the waiter came to tell them their table was ready. When they were seated Marc smiled at her, handing her the menu.

'Choose something you really like. This is a special occasion.'

She looked at him over the top of the large, glossy card. 'Oh—why?'

He smiled. 'I'll tell you later.'

As they ate he talked about his home in Guernsey and how much he looked forward to living there again.

'You could hardly have a more stark contrast,' he told her. 'The industrial Midlands and the Channel Islands are about as different as they can be.'

'I've lived in the Midlands all my life,' Abigail said. 'Dad never had time to take me for holidays. I used to go and stay with an aunt in Skegness when he felt I needed a change of air, but I always missed him too much to really enjoy it.'

'You'd love Guernsey,' he told her. 'Having the sea all round always made me feel safe, yet free at the same time when I was a child. The air is so clean and in summer the scent of flowers is everywhere.'

'It sounds beautiful,' she said wistfully.

They were at the coffee stage. Abigail poured out two cups from the pot the waiter brought, and as she passed one across the table to him he took her hand and held it firmly. She looked up into the golden eyes and felt her heart melt.

'I told you that this was a special occasion, Abby,' he said quietly. 'Would you like to know why?'

'Yes—if you want to tell me.'

His eyes held hers. 'I'm going to be married.'

It took every shred of her control not to let her face

slip—not to show the shock she felt. 'I—see.' She swallowed hard. 'Is it—to anyone I know?'

He smiled and his eyes seemed to draw her closer as he said softly, 'Oh yes—you see, I'm going to marry you, Abby—if you'll have me, that is!'

CHAPTER TWO

IT SEEMED an eternity before Abigail found her voice. Time seemed to stand still. The other diners in the restaurant melted away as she stared incredulously at Marc, her throat constricting and her blue eyes round with surprise. Marc poured the last of the wine into her glass, touching her hand as he passed it to her.

'Darling, I'm sorry. I didn't mean to shock you. Is the prospect of marrying me *so* awful?'

Her hand shook as she raised the glass to her lips and took a sip. 'I—don't know what to say,' she whispered. 'It—it isn't some kind of joke—is it?'

He frowned, his eyes darkening as they looked into hers. 'I don't make jokes like that!' He glanced around him. 'Look, if you've finished your coffee, shall we go?'

She nodded gratefully and rose from the table. 'Yes, I'll get my coat. See you outside.' He grasped her arm as she passed him, looking down at her in a way that turned her knees to water.

'You won't run away, will you?'

She looked up at him in surprise. 'No, I won't run away.'

In the cloakroom she was thankful to find herself alone. She leaned her burning forehead against the cool pink tiles, convinced that she was dreaming all this and only needed something to waken her. It was so bizarre— Marc asking her to marry him out of the blue like this. What was she to say to him? Would he expect her to return to Guernsey with him when he went? Give up her job and go with him—just like that? She looked at herself in the mirror and saw two huge blue eyes in a white, shocked face.

'Would you really do it—*marry* him?' she asked herself aloud. But the question was superfluous. How could she let him go out of her life now? It might take a little planning—a *lot* of planning—but no considering at all. It was like a miracle—almost too good to be true!

After a little breathing space and a touch of lipstick she felt more composed, though when she saw him waiting for her in the entrance hall, standing there so tall and straight with his back towards her, she felt her heart lurch again. He turned and saw her and his face broke into a smile.

'Ah, there you are. I was beginning to wonder.' He slipped an arm round her waist. 'Let's get out of here, shall we?'

In the warm darkness of the car he reached out to pull her into his arms. 'Darling Abby—was it such a blow? I'm sorry I asked you so abruptly. I just didn't know how else to do it. Do you forgive me?'

She nodded, her head bumping against his shoulder.

He cupped her chin, raising her head so that he could kiss her, and she felt the familiar dizziness swallowing her up. Moving his head back a little, he looked into her eyes.

'You haven't given me your answer yet.'

She caught her breath. 'You—you've never given me any clue. You've never said you—loved me, even.'

He laughed gently, shaking his head at her reprovingly. 'Couldn't you tell? I thought women always knew these things instinctively!'

'But you're always so nice to everyone. I thought—' The rest of the sentence was lost as he kissed her again.

'Not *this* nice, I promise you,' he said teasingly. 'I might as well warn you, Abby—I'm not taking no for an answer. Ideally, of course, I'd like us to be married almost at once, so that you could come back to Guernsey with me when I go. But if I have to wait for you, I will—not for *too* long though. Patience isn't my strong suit, not where you're concerned, anyway.'

She leaned against him weakly, feeling like a leaf blown in the wind. He seemed to have it all worked out—to take it for granted that she loved him. Had she been that obvious? 'I—I'd like a little time to think about it, Marc,' she told him. 'There would be so much to take into consideration—my job, everything.'

He held her away from him, searching her eyes. 'Does that mean that the answer is yes?'

She bit her lip. 'Marc! I don't know—you haven't asked me if I love *you*. It all seems the wrong way round. So—so—'

'So unromantic?' He pulled her close again. 'I promise you, darling, that there'll be all the romance you want when we get home to Guernsey. I've rushed you off your feet, I know. But it's only because of the circumstances—the lack of time.' He looked down at her. 'Fancy not knowing that I loved you! It was almost love at first sight. The moment I first set eyes on you with those huge kitten blue eyes and that hair—' He picked up a strand of it and held it against his cheek. 'Exactly the colour of butterscotch.'

Abigail laughed. 'Butterscotch! I've always thought of it as mouse!' Her laughter released the tensions. It washed over her like a refreshing wave and she wound her arms around his neck and drew his head down to hers. 'Oh, Marc, I do love you so, and of course I'll marry you if you really want me—just as soon as I can!'

Marc was on call that weekend, which meant that they couldn't go out. But on Sunday evening they were both invited to dinner with Dr Bill Curtis, the senior partner in the group practice. His wife, Helen, rang Abigail early on Saturday morning.

'My dear, Marc has just told us your news. Congratulations! Bill and I are so pleased. We'd like you both to come to dinner tomorrow evening if it isn't too short notice. I know that neither of you has parents here to give you a little celebration, so we'd like to do it for you.'

'That's very kind of you,' Abigail told her. 'I'm sure we'd both love to come, but please don't go to a lot of trouble.'

'It'll only be the four of us,' Helen told her. 'I did ring round the others, but they all seem to have something arranged for this weekend. They all send their congratulations though.'

Abigail was relieved. She hated the idea of a fuss. Besides, she still hadn't got used to the idea of being engaged. Would people think it odd, she wondered, their getting married in such haste?

But she was wrong. Helen seemed to see nothing strange in their surprise engagement when she greeted Abigail on Sunday evening. She took her upstairs to take off her coat, apologising for Marc, who had been called out.

'It's a child with a temperature; nothing serious, I'm sure. He'll be back soon. I'm glad of this opportunity to have a little talk with you alone, dear. I've been thinking—why not have your wedding reception here? Unless of course you have other plans.' She had seen the look of apprehension on Abigail's face. 'Perhaps you want to wait and see what your mother thinks—perhaps she—'

'Oh no.' Abigail shook her head. 'I'm sure she won't

have time to arrange anything. Perhaps Marc has told you that she's a journalist—the editor of a magazine. She's going to be furious that I haven't given her more notice as it is.'

Helen nodded understandingly. 'I dare say, but it can't be helped under the circumstances, can it? Now, the lounge downstairs is large enough to accommodate about thirty people, I would say, and if the weather is nice we can open the french windows and let them overflow on to the lawn. What do you say?'

Abigail laughed breathlessly. 'It sounds wonderful, but I haven't a clue how many people we shall ask. Marc and I haven't talked about the actual wedding yet.'

'Well, have a talk with him and let me know.' Helen smiled. 'I must admit that the idea gives me quite a thrill. Having two great football-playing sons, I'd quite given up the hope that I'd one day have the chance to put on a wedding. Bill and I will simply revel in it—in fact, I rather think that Bill is secretly hoping to be asked to give the bride away,' she confided.

Once more Abigail had the feeling that life was carrying her along. It was an odd sensation, like riding some crazy merry-go-round. Half of her wanted it to stop, while the other half of her was enjoying the stomach-churning excitement.

Marc arrived while they were having a pre-dinner drink. He stood in the doorway, watching Abigail for a moment, taking in the slim figure and long legs. She was wearing the red dress bought for Jennifer's party, having had no time to buy anything new. He hadn't seen it before and he liked the way it brought out the creami-ness of her skin. She turned and saw his admiring look and a warm coral flush coloured her cheeks. He held out his hands to her.

'You look lovely. Sorry I wasn't here when you arrived. I expect Helen explained.'

She went to him. 'I expect that's something I shall have to get used to. I hope the child is all right.'

He kissed her briefly. 'Suspected chicken-pox. There are a few cases about.'

Helen marshalled them. 'Well, now that Marc is here we can eat. We'd better make a start before the telephone rings again. Do let's go in, all of you.'

Dr Bill Curtis was a warm, good-natured man who adored his home and family. Tall and grey-haired, he smiled benignly at his wife across the heads of his junior partner and his fiancée as they all sat down to dinner.

'It's good to see you getting yourself settled, Marc,' he said approvingly as he helped himself to vegetables. 'There's nothing like a good family life, you know, especially for a family doctor.' He sighed. 'The only bad thing about it is that we'll be losing two such good people.' He smiled at Abigail. 'You're both going to be sorely missed, you know. I've had some very good reports of you, my dear, both from the patients and the staff at the Wellbourne. Will you be continuing with your work when you get to Guernsey?'

Abigail opened her mouth to tell him that she hoped to, but before she could speak Marc said, 'I think Abigail will find most of her time occupied. Besides, I doubt if there will be any vacancies.'

Bill shook his head. 'That will be a great pity.' He smiled at Abigail across the table. 'A great loss to the profession, if I may say so.'

Abigail stared at Marc. 'I would like to carry on nursing—for a while at least. I'm sure I can make myself useful, even if it's only helping with the family practice.'

Marc looked up and their eyes met. He smiled

indulgently. 'That would be marvellous, darling—until you have your hands full with our own family, that is.'

Bill and Helen laughed gently and Abigail felt the warm colour creeping up her neck. There was so much that she and Marc hadn't discussed—so much he was simply taking for granted. Would they see eye to eye on the important issues of life?

Helen served the sweet course and Bill turned to Abigail. 'What do you think of the scheme we're running here of short-stay confinements?' he asked her. 'I think myself it's the perfect compromise between hospital and home births. And I do feel that it's much nicer for the patient to have the same midwife looking after her throughout, don't you?'

'Oh yes.' Abigail leaned forward eagerly. 'It must have been so bewildering for a young mother to be whisked into hospital to be delivered by complete strangers—frustrating for the district midwife too, not to see the case through to its conclusion. I feel the scheme works very well.'

'So do I,' Marc agreed. 'My cousin, Leslie, hopes to specialise in obstetrics and is hoping to get a similar scheme going at home.'

As Helen brought in the coffee, Bill raised his glass and proposed a toast. 'To Marc and Abigail. May life be good to them.'

Helen echoed the sentiment and Abigail looked up, meeting Marc's eyes. As they looked at her they were tender and smiling and she felt reassured. Surely there would be nothing they couldn't work out together? He was so kind   wasn't that the opinion of everyone who knew him?

Bill caught the look that passed between them and cleared his throat. 'Now look, you two—this is a pretty special evening. Why don't you take Abigail up to the flat for a while, Marc? There must be so much for you to talk about. I'll take your calls for you for the next couple of hours.'

Marc's flat was at the top of the elegant Edwardian house. It had originally been made for Helen's mother who had lived with the Curtis family until she died, two years before Marc joined the practice. It was the perfect flat for a bachelor doctor; self-contained, neat and comfortable, with its own separate entrance at the rear of the house.

'There was even a stair-lift when I first came here,' Marc told her as he opened the door. 'I was quite sorry when it was taken out. There are times when I'd be quite glad of it!' He closed the door behind them and pulled her into his arms, kissing her lingeringly.

'Mmm—I've been wanting to do that all evening,' he said against her hair. 'I expect Bill could see that when he suggested we came up here for a while. Understanding old boy, isn't he?' He sank on to the settee and pulled her down with him, settling her head comfortably on his shoulder.

Abigail slid her arms around him. 'I felt awful, rushing away after the lovely dinner Helen had cooked for us. It seemed so ungrateful.'

He laughed gently, kissing her forehead. 'Not at all. Helen was expecting it. She knew I wanted to give you this.' He took a small box out of his pocket and gave it to her. She opened it and found inside a beautiful antique ring set with a large ruby, surrounded by diamonds. Marc took it from her and slipped it on to the third finger of her left hand.

'There—a perfect fit if ever I saw one. That must be a good omen, wouldn't you say?'

Abigail held out her hand to admire the ruby's fiery sparkle. 'Oh, Marc—it's beautiful! Where did you find it?' she breathed.

'It's a family heirloom,' he told her. 'Always passed on to the eldest son's wife. It's been in the family for quite a few generations, though of course it's been re-set several times.'

She looked up at him happily, her eyes shining. 'I love it, Marc. I'll take great care of it always.'

He drew her close. 'And I'll take great care of you, darling.'

Marc's kisses made her drowsy. 'Tell me about your family,' she asked, settling her head more comfortably in the hollow of his shoulder. He sighed.

'There isn't much to tell. There have been DeLisles on Guernsey for about three hundred years, but now there are only three of us left.' He twisted his head to smile down at her. 'Four soon—counting you.'

'And have you always been doctors?'

'No. That started in the eighteenth century,' he told her. 'I'm afraid the original settler who came over from France was the black sheep of the family—a privateer on the run. That branch of the family was considered beyond the pale until the French Revolution, when they opened their doors to their fleeing refugee cousins and so redeemed themselves.'

Abigail smiled, a little in awe. 'I'd no idea you had such a fascinating background. I'm afraid that mine is very mundane by comparison.'

He lifted her chin to smile down at her. 'It isn't your background I'm interested in, darling. Which reminds me—Bill said he'd take my calls for the next couple of hours. I can't think why we're wasting it talking about my boring family history!'

She tried to free herself from his encircling arms. 'Marc, there is so much we have to talk about. Before you came back, when I first arrived here, Helen was talking about having our wedding reception here—then there is the question of when I should give in my notice and—and—' Her voice trailed off as he pressed her gently back against the cushions, his eyes mocking her tenderly as his fingers traced a line from her ear to the hollow of her throat. Bending his head he followed the line with his lips, sending tiny shivers of ecstasy down her spine. Lifting her arm he pressed his lips against the soft skin inside her wrist, then slowly began to unfasten the tiny buttons at the front of her dress. His lips found hers and she surrendered with a sigh, lost in their magic as his hand found and caressed one breast.

'Tell me you love me again,' he whispered, his lips moving sensuously against hers. 'I'll never tire of hearing you say it.'

'I love you—' She gasped a little as she felt him sliding the dress from her shoulders, caressing her skin with seductive fingers. 'Marc—' Her heartbeat quickened. 'Marc, please, I—' But his lips were on hers again, hard and demanding, parting her own to claim her completely. She wanted him with a fierceness that took her by surprise. Suddenly the telephone on the table beside the settee jangled abruptly. Marc went on kissing her for a moment, then released her with a sigh.

'Damn!' he said with feeling as he reached out to pick up the receiver. Abigail could hear Bill's voice quite clearly at the other end of the line. He sounded apologetic.

'I'm sorry, Marc, old son. It's old Mr Freeman over at Warden's Cross. He's had another attack and it seems he's asking for you specially. I thought you might want to go.'

Marc sighed and ran a hand through his hair, smiling ruefully at Abigail. 'Yes—yes, of course, Bill. Thanks for letting me know. I'm on my way.' He put down the telephone and looked at her thoughtfully. 'Will you wait here till I get back?'

She glanced at her watch and shook her head. 'No. I'd better not. I have to be up early in the morning to catch the London train.' She stood up and went to the mirror over the fireplace to tidy herself. For a moment he sat watching her, then he went and stood behind her, pulling her back against him and smiling at her reflection in the mirror.

'I'm always rushing you into things, aren't I? Poor little Abby.' He bent to kiss her neck just under her ear, and she turned in his arms, her eyes sparkling up at him.

'It must be all that Gallic blood coursing round in your veins—all the wickedness from your pirate ancestor coming out.'

His arms tightened round her, the corners of his mouth lifting. 'And does it put you off?' he teased.

She shook her head, the heavy hair swinging. 'Not on your life, Dr DeLisle!'

They ran down the two flights of stairs together, laughing like children, and got into their respective cars. Marc bent to put his head in at the window.

'I'll be glad when you've handed in the keys for this,' he said. 'When I can have you all to myself!' He kissed her. 'Have a good day with your mother tomorrow, darling—see you soon.'

She watched as he swung his long legs into his own car and drove away. Then, switching on her engine, she began the drive back to Weston Rise thoughtfully.

When she was in his arms she would do anything in the whole world for Marc. But how much was he prepared to compromise for her? He said he would be glad when she had handed in the keys to her car, but to her it symbolised her status and independence. A tiny doubt pricked at the back of her mind; was she letting her heart rule her head? Then she thought of the way Marc could make her laugh—the heady sensation when he kissed her and the shattering intensity with which she had wanted him earlier this evening. She sighed. What was a car, a mere chunk of metal, compared to all that?

The following morning she almost overslept and had a frantic rush to catch the London train. Although it was still very early the day promised to be fine, and as she stood on the platform among the glum, Monday-faced commuters she felt light-hearted, the doubts of the previous evening quite forgotten. The train was announced and glided into the station. Abigail found a seat by the window and watched as the factories and terraces of Victorian houses that made up the older part of the town formed the familiar panorama.

Soon I'll be leaving all this, she told herself as the train picked up speed and the grimy back-to-backs gave way to the shiny suburbs and then to green fields. She tried to examine her feelings on the subject. Rinkley might not be the most beautiful place in the world, but it was home to her. Guernsey . . . What would it be like living there—being Marc's wife and a member of an old and distinguished family? It would be a whole new way of life. The thought of it sent a little quiver of excitement through her. 'Mrs Marcus DeLisle', she said to herself experimentally. 'Abigail DeLisle.' It sounded very grand. Would she be able to live up to it? How would

Marc's relatives—few though they were—take to his sudden and unexpected marriage to a complete stranger?

At the back of her mind Marc's words to Bill Curtis at dinner last night jabbed persistently. 'I think Abigail will find most of her time occupied.' He had been so dismissive—as though her career had been merely a marking of time until marriage and was of no importance. Irritably she thrust the thought from her, refusing to allow anything to spoil her happiness. The sky was blue, the sun was shining, and she had the day off. But best of all, tonight she would return to Marc, the man she loved—her future husband.

Jennifer Brent's mews flat was in Kensington. Bay trees in tubs stood on either side of the white-painted front door leading up to it, and at the first floor windows crimson geraniums and blue lobelia tumbled in bright profusion out of the window boxes. Jennifer came to the door in her housecoat although it was now after ten o'clock. At forty-eight she looked at least ten years younger, her figure slim and her skin smooth and unlined. She kissed Abigail warmly.

'Lovely to see you, darling. Do come up. You're just in time for some breakfast.'

Abigail didn't argue. Having overslept, she hadn't had time for more than a snatched cup of coffee. In the trim, gadget-filled kitchen, Jennifer chattered brightly as she poured orange juice and popped bacon under the grill.

'Isn't it a lovely day? What shall we do with it? It's too nice for a matinée or an art gallery for shopping too, I suppose. What about Hyde Park—lazing in the sun?'

'I'd rather like to go shopping,' Abigail said. 'As a

matter of fact, there's something I want you to help me choose.'

Jennifer turned to her with a bright smile, pausing as she spooned coffee into the filter. 'Oh yes, and what would that be?'

'A wedding dress actually—going-away outfit too, I suppose.' She hadn't meant to blurt it out like that and the moment the words had escaped she bit her tongue. It was the kind of thing that was guaranteed to annoy Jennifer. The smile drained from her face as she turned to stare at her daughter, coffee jar and spoon still in her hands.

'I take it you *are* joking! Though I really can't say I think much of your sense of humour, Abby.'

Abigail sighed and sat down at the table. 'I'm sorry. I really didn't mean to break the news to you like that. It is true though. I am getting married—and very soon, too.'

Jennifer looked at her shrewdly. 'I do hope you haven't been behaving stupidly.'

It was Abigail's turn to be irritated. 'Not unless you call falling in love being stupid,' she retorted. 'He's called Marcus DeLisle and he's a doctor in a group practice in Rinkley, though his home is in the Channel Islands. His father has recently died and left him the family practice over there. He has to go home and take up the reins as soon as he can. That's the reason for the sudden decision and the haste.'

Jennifer sat down looking somewhat mollified. 'I see. But why haven't I heard about him before? Obviously you must have known him for ages.'

'Not really,' Abigail admitted. 'In fact we've only been out together about half a dozen times. I knew I was falling in love with him from the first though—and it seems it was mutual.' This last assertion came out rather defiantly, and Jennifer got up to attend to the food looking thoughtful.

'Look, Abby, I know we've never been close—not really close, I mean, in the way that mothers and daughters usually are—but I hope you'll allow me to advise you, even if it's only as an older woman to a younger one.' She put the plate of bacon and eggs in front of Abigail and sat down again opposite her. 'I know you're a doctor's daughter, but I wonder if you have any idea of what it can be like to be a doctor's wife?'

Abigail sighed. 'Of course I have. I was brought up in that atmosphere. I've worked in it too. I know all the pressures.'

'As a participant, yes. Being a *wife* is somewhat different, you know.' Jennifer raised her eyes ceilingwards. 'I lost count of the number of parties we had to cry off at the last minute because of some rotten emergency—the number of dinners I gave for your father, only to have to make his excuses and entertain his boring colleagues myself.'

'Obviously you and Dad weren't suited to each other,' Abigail protested. 'Marc and I are. I understand his work in a way that you were never able to, not being part of it.'

'Then there is the small matter of one's identity,' Jennifer went on, nibbling a piece of toast. 'Your father just never took my career seriously. He seemed to think that the whole of my energy should be devoted to hanging around waiting for the few precious moments he could spare me and being his general dogsbody— answering the telephone and administering to tiresome patients who most of the time had totally imaginary illnesses! I can't think how I stuck it for the ten years I did!' She threw a look at Abigail. 'If it hadn't been for you, I would have walked out years before. It isn't much fun, you know, sharing your husband with about two hundred demanding people who seem to think they have more right to him than you have!'

Abigail cringed inwardly. She had heard it all so many times before. 'But when you work *together*, as a partnership,' she began, but Jennifer waved a hand at her dismissively.

'That particular partnership was distinctly one-sided!' She leaned across the table. 'You see, I felt that your father never really *needed* me. At least, he did, but not in the way I wanted to be needed—for myself, as someone unique and special in his life. The things I did for him could be done by anyone, and in the end I decided that I'd be better employed somewhere else.' She gave a bitter little laugh. 'And I think you have to agree, darling, that I was right.'

'Yes, but that's only *your* experience,' Abigail insisted. 'You're not really trying to put me off marriage, or Marc, are you?'

Jennifer looked at the crestfallen face and smiled, relenting. 'I'm sorry, darling.' She reached out to touch Abigail's hand. 'Of course I'm not. I only want you to be very sure and very happy.'

'I am,' Abigail told her. They smiled at each other and Jennifer took a deep breath.

'That's all right then. Now—tell me all your plans. Heavens! I shall have to start thinking about what I'm to wear too. Mother of the bride! How important it sounds.'

'We haven't set an actual date yet,' Abigail told her. 'But it must be within the month. Marc wants to get home as soon as he can. I expect I shall be giving in my notice tomorrow. Helen Curtis has offered—' She stopped speaking as she caught sight of her mother's face. 'What is it—is something wrong?'

Jennifer groaned. 'Within the month! Your timing, my love, is the absolute end! The reason I asked you to come up for the day was partly so that I could tell you my news. The company is sending me over to the States to study American teenage magazines. There's a good chance of a new one being launched here and it's to be my baby. I'm off this weekend and I shall be away for six weeks!'

Abigail tried hard not to show her disappointment. Clearly it was an important step up for Jennifer, but to have neither of her parents present at her wedding seemed so bleak, especially when Marc would have no relatives there either. It looked very much as though she would have to rely on Helen Curtis's kindness and generosity.

Jennifer looked at her, her eyes clouded. 'Isn't there anything we can do? I suppose there isn't the slightest chance of you postponing the wedding?'

Abigail shook her head. 'Marc wants me to be with him when he leaves. I want it too.'

'Naturally.' Jennifer smiled. 'Ah—what it is to be young and in love. Oh well, it can't be helped. You'll just have to send me dozens of photographs and save me a piece of cake—don't forget that. Now, if we're to get to the West End shops before lunch I'd better get dressed.'

In spite of the disappointment, Abigail managed to enjoy her day. Jennifer insisted on buying her wedding outfit and they chose it together—Jennifer suggesting a pastel colour rather than white.

'With your colouring it washes you out, darling.'

Abigail had to admit that she was right. Whatever else, Jennifer had impeccable taste in clothes. As soon as she slipped the dress on they both knew that it was the one. A pale peachy pink, the soft material of the bodice clung to her, moulding her slim figure as though it had been specially made. The skirt, a mass of tiny pleats, swirled about her hips romantically, and they came out of the shop feeling well pleased with themselves.

'A hat! You must have a hat. The most dreamy, fairy-tale one we can find, and I know *just* where to find it!' Jennifer whirled Abigail into a taxi and gave the address of a tiny Bond Street boutique where the milliner was an old friend. She was right. They both saw it as soon as they got out of the taxi. Right in the centre of the window was the 'dream hat' Jennifer had been looking for, but when Abigail saw the price she gasped.

'You can't! I won't let you!' But Jennifer brushed her protests aside.

'I don't care what you say. You're not robbing me of the privilege of buying my only daughter's wedding hat, so don't dare try!' She stood back, regarding her daughter with misty eyes. 'Oh dear, maybe it's just as well I won't be there. I'd probably weep buckets and ruin my make-up!'

Abigail's reflection looked back at her from the gilt-framed mirror. The wide brim of the hat was covered in layers of creamy chiffon that lifted gently as she moved—the crown trimmed with delicate wild rose-buds. It was the perfect frame for her small oval face.

Finally they stopped for tea, sitting exhausted, surrounded by their parcels. After she had ordered, Jennifer took out her cheque book.

'Your wedding present—much more sensible for you to choose something you both like,' she announced, signing the cheque with a flourish. Abigail looked at it in surprise.

'It's too much—please.'

'Not it isn't.' Jennifer pushed her hand away. 'I haven't done much for you over the years, Abby. It hasn't been entirely my fault, but I've felt it just the same—perhaps more keenly than you think. And now I can't even be at your wedding. At least allow me to do this one small thing.'

Abigail's throat tightened as she pressed her mother's hand. 'Maybe when we're settled and you're back in this country you could come over and visit,' she whispered. Jennifer's eyes widened.

'Just you try and stop me! I want to meet this new son-in-law of mine as soon as I can, and don't you forget it!' She pulled a face. 'Good Lord! I've just thought— I'm about to become a mother-in-law! Every time I hear one of those ghastly jokes I shall have to identify with it!'

They took a taxi to King's Cross and Jennifer hugged her daughter warmly as she said goodbye.

'Let me know the date of the wedding as soon as you can—and the time, of course, so that I can be thinking about you.' She waved from the taxi window and Abigail was left standing on the pavement, alone again, watching her mother's waving hand until the rush-hour traffic swallowed the taxi up and she was gone.

The train she caught was a slow one, giving her plenty of time to think. Jennifer's words came back to her and she thought carefully about her parents' stormy relationship, remembering all too well the quarrels and the brooding resentment that had hung like a cloud over her early childhood. She and Marc would not be like that— of course they wouldn't. Her mother and father were in love once, just as she and Marc were, but the difference was their incompatibility. Jennifer had always loved to be the one in charge—organising and running things.

She was good at her job and during the time when Abigail was a baby she had missed it, resented being a 'dogsbody' as she had called it. Abigail would be a true partner to her husband, helping and sharing in his work. He would never take her for granted—would he?

To her delighted surprise, he was waiting for her when she stepped off the train. She rushed into his arms.

'Marc! How could you have known which one I'd be on?'

He kissed her. 'I didn't. I was prepared to wait, but I was lucky as it happened. You were on the first one to arrive.' He took her parcels from her. 'Have you had a good day? It looks as though you've bought up half of London!'

She laughed, linking her arm through his as they went to the car park.

'Not quite. It is important though—my wedding dress.'

He smiled at her. 'Ah—and do I get a private modelling show?'

'You certainly do not!' she told him indignantly. 'Don't you know that's bad luck? You'll have to wait until the big day.'

They were standing by his car now and Marc opened the passenger door for her. As he seated himself beside her and fastened his belt, he smiled. 'That reminds me. The wedding date—it's May the thirtieth. A Saturday. I've applied for the licence, seen the vicar and checked with Helen too. She says that'll be fine. She's already started to make plans.'

Abigail was silent as she fought down her resentment and disappointment. Marc glanced at her.

'What is it—anything wrong?'

She bit her lip. 'It's awfully soon, isn't it? Only two weeks away. And what about my job?'

'Ah—no need to worry about that either. I've arranged everything. Everyone was very understanding when I explained the situation. Old Sister Gregson, whose place you took, is willing to come back until another midwife can be appointed.'

'I see. So it's all cut and dried?' Abigail said stiffly.

'Yes—aren't you pleased?' He glanced at her again, his smile fading as he saw her expression.

'Didn't it occur to you to ask me first?' She looked around her. 'And where are you going? This isn't the way to Weston Rise.'

'I thought we'd have a quiet dinner somewhere, to celebrate.'

'Are you ever going to ask me about *anything*?' Her voice was shrill, almost panicky, and she bit her lip, near to tears. Without another word Marc turned into a small lane and stopped the car, turning to her, his eyes concerned.

'Darling, what is it? Did you quarrel with your mother? Has something happened to upset you?'

She felt a prickle of irritation. Why did he naturally assume that if she was upset it must be someone else's fault?

He picked up her hand and held it between both of his. 'Look, you're tired. If you don't want to go out it's all right. Would you like me to take you home?'

He was making her feel churlish and ungrateful. 'I—am a bit tired,' she said, her resolve weakening. 'Marc about the wedding arrangements. Couldn't you have consulted me about them? After all, it does concern me too. And as for giving in my notice *for* me— what will they think? It makes me seem so feeble having someone else to do it for me.'

He laughed, bending his head to kiss her gently. 'I'm not *someone else*, darling—I'm your future husband!'

Her eyes flashed at him. 'And you think that makes it all right, do you? Am I to have my mind made up about everything?'

He stared at her in surprise. 'Aren't you being just a little unreasonable, darling? After all, the circumstances are unusual. We just don't have the time that people usually do. I thought you'd be pleased that I'd managed to get so much organised on one day.'

She sighed. How could she explain to him that she felt her life was being taken over—that she was being carried along on something that felt uncomfortably like a tidal wave? He tipped up her chin to look at her.

'You're not regretting all this, are you, Abby? If you'd rather wait—'

She threw her arms around his neck and hid her face against his shoulder. 'No. I'm sorry. I'm just being silly, I suppose. It's only that—'

'Only that it's all been a bit sudden,' he finished for her. 'A bit overwhelming. I understand, darling, of course I do.' He held her a little away from him. 'You haven't changed your mind, have you—about loving me?'

She smiled and shook her head. In all the tangle of bewildering doubts, that was the one thing she was a hundred per cent sure of.

'That's all that really matters.' He kissed the tip of her nose. 'Everything will work itself out, just wait and see. By the way, what did your mother think of your news?'

'She was a little taken aback, though she did enjoy helping me choose my dress. The bad news is that she won't be able to come to the wedding. She's off to

America at the end of this week and she'll be there for six weeks.'

He pulled her close. 'I knew something had happened to upset you. Look, suppose we pick up a take-away meal somewhere and go back to your place?'

She looked up at him. 'Could we? That would be lovely.'

They ate their Chinese meal in Abigail's small living-room, sitting comfortably on the settee with trays on their laps. When they had cleared away the remains, Marc chose a record from her collection—a selection of romantic piano pieces. He took off his jacket and sank into a corner of the settee, holding out his arms to her. As he leaned back, eyes half-closed as he listened to the music, she studied his face—the firm jawline and fascinating cleft chin, the sensuously moulded lips and strong straight nose. Between his brows was a single, deeply etched line, telling of long hours of study and concentration.

She lifted her hand to smooth back the thick brown hair from his forehead and he caught it, holding the fingertips to his lips briefly, then rubbing his cheek against the palm. She felt her heartbeat quicken as he reached out to cradle the back of her head with one hand, drawing her closer. When he kissed her she melted, all her earlier resentment evaporating as his lips moved sensuously against hers, experimentally at first, as though testing her mood, then more deeply, stirring her senses. His fingers slid inside the open neck of her shirt, stroking her seductively. Bending, he pressed his lips against the little fluttering pulse at the base of her throat.

'Your skin is like satin,' he murmured, finding her mouth again. She trembled as her lips parted beneath his and she clung to him, her heart thudding wildly. Her whole being cried out for him as she thrilled to the answering beat of his heart against hers. With trembling fingers she began to undo the buttons of his shirt, but his hand closed over hers and he put her gently from him. She stared at him mutely.

'I'm—going to say good night now, Abby,' he said huskily.

She shook her head. 'Why? What's the matter?'

He smiled ruefully and rubbed his forehead against hers. 'Absolutely nothing is the matter, darling. At this moment I want to make love to you more than anything else in the world—but I'm not going to. It's such a short time to wait and I want everything to be perfect. I want us to be at home—at King's Rock—in our own house with the sound of the sea in our ears.' He stood up, drawing her to her feet too, looking down into her eyes. 'You do understand, darling? I want it all to be right.'

She nodded dumbly, trying not to let him see the agony of yearning she felt. He kissed her briefly.

'Don't come to the door with me. Go to bed now. You've had a long day and you'll be on duty again tomorrow. Good night, darling.'

After he had gone she stood for a long time, staring unseeingly out of the window. Her skin still tingled from his touch. Why couldn't he have seen how much she needed him tonight? To have stayed together would have put everything right—would have allayed all the doubts that had tormented her, all her fears for the future—fears that were mounting alarmingly as each day passed.

CHAPTER THREE

'YOUR WIFE is doing fine, Mr Palmer.' Abigail smiled reassuringly at the pale young man standing anxiously at the bottom of the stairs. 'It'll be some time yet before she is ready to go to the hospital though. I'll call back again in a couple of hours.'

'But the pain—it seems so bad,' he protested. 'Isn't there anything at all I can get her? Some aspirin?'

Abigail shook her head. 'I'm afraid not. Everything is quite normal. Try not to worry. Why don't you make her a cup of tea?'

She left the young man filling the kettle at the kitchen sink and looking desperately worried. If only she could have stayed with him and his young wife a little longer—but she was still only half-way through her morning rounds.

Getting back into the car, she glanced at her watch—almost twelve. She was very behind now. She would have her work cut out to see everyone before lunch—and she would have to arrange for another midwife to take her place this afternoon at the ante-natal clinic. Mrs Palmer would be needing her before it was over, if she was any judge.

The next two calls were routine and straightforward. Two recently discharged mothers who were coping well. Abigail went home and rang to arrange for a replacement for the afternoon clinic, snatched a quick lunch and then made the remainder of the calls left over from the morning. There had been a message the previous day from John Jeffreys, whose baby daughter was now three weeks old. Abigail had stopped calling on Janet ten days ago.

'If you could just call in, sort of casually,' John had said hesitantly. 'I know how busy you must be—it's an imposition to ask you really, but she's been so depressed.'

It wasn't an unusual story, but he had sounded so worried that Abigail had decided to call even if it was only to reassure him. It was two o'clock when she pushed open the gate of the pretty white-painted cottage and walked up the path. Baby Abigail slept soundly in her smart new pram on the neat lawn under a lilac tree and Janet could be seen at the kitchen window. At once Abigail could see what her husband had meant. Janet's face was pale and drawn and her eyes were suspiciously red. Abigail tapped on the door and opened it.

'May I come in?' she asked cheerfully.

Janet looked surprised and confused. 'Oh! I—wasn't expecting you.'

'Just thought I'd pop in and see how you were as I was passing,' Abigail said diplomatically. 'How have you been?'

Janet stared at her for a moment, then sat down heavily on a chair and burst into tears. 'John rang you, didn't he? Told you I couldn't cope—that I was hopeless at being a mother?'

Abigail took off her hat and sat down opposite Janet. 'All right—yes, he did ring. But he didn't say any of those things. He's worried because you seem so low. Now, how about telling me all about?'

Janet rose to her feet hurriedly. 'I can't—not now. It's the baby's feed time.'

Very gently Abigail pushed her back into the chair. 'I

can't hear her crying, can you? When I passed her pram on the way in she was sleeping like a log—the picture of contentment. Tell you what—how about putting the kettle on for a cup of tea? Would you like me to make it?'

Janet shrugged. 'If you like.' She made no attempt to get up from the table, allowing Abigail to find the teapot and brew the tea. She looked ten years older. Gone was the radiant glow she had worn like a halo after the baby's birth. Abigail regarded her shrewdly as she poured the tea and passed her a cup.

'Now, what is it? There's no problem that isn't made smaller by sharing it, you know.'

Helpless tears slid down Janet's face. 'I'm hopeless,' she said. 'I have been from the start. To begin with, once I got home I couldn't feed her any more.'

'Well, that's no tragedy. I knew about that anyway.' Abigail said lightly. 'It didn't seem to bother you at the time. And we got her on to a bottle without any trouble, didn't we?'

'At first, but now she seems to cry all night. She's usually sick after a feed too, and she's got—she's got— nappy rash!' The last words brought forth fresh sobs and Mrs Jeffreys laid her head down on her arms despairingly. 'I should never have had her. I'm too old. I'll ruin John's life and hers too!'

Abigail stood up and slipped an arm round the shaking shoulders. 'Come along now, Janet. Drink your tea, then I'll have a look at Baby. You've got everything blown up out of all proportion. It's probably only a change of food she needs. Babies are like us, you know, not everything suits them. I've got some samples in the car. We'll sort something out for her. I've got some cream for the rash too.' She patted Janet's shoulder. 'As for you—it's my guess that all you really need is a good night's sleep!'

Half an hour later she stopped the car to make a quick call to John Jeffreys at his office.

'I've seen your wife, Mr Jeffreys,' she told him. 'Nothing to worry about. Just an attack of baby blues. Lots of women get them. We've sorted out the feeding problem, I hope, and the rash too. But what I'd like you to do is to put your wife to bed in the spare room and take over the baby for her—just for the weekend so that she can have a couple of nights of undisturbed sleep. I'm sure you'll find that will make all the difference.'

'Of course I will.' John sounded relieved. 'I know she's been trying to do too much—driving herself too hard, almost as though she were trying to prove something. I'll certainly take the baby over for the weekend—if she'll let me.'

'She'll let you,' Abigail assured him. 'I've told her I'm suggesting it. She seemed quite relieved to have someone to make the decision for her.'

When she arrived back at the Palmer's house the young husband met her at the door, his face white and anxious.

'Oh, thank goodness you're here, Nurse. Pam is having the pains very fast now. I'm sure it must be time to take her to the hospital.'

Abigail made a quick examination, then telephoned the Wellbourne to tell them that she and her patient were on their way. She glanced at the young man. 'Are you going to be present at the birth?'

He tried hard to smile. 'Well, I said I would be—if she needs me.'

'Fine. Get her into the car then and on your way. I'll be following you up.'

In spite of young Mr Palmer's anxiety, it was another three hours before his baby son was born. Fighting off his apprehension, he had allowed himself to be masked and gowned to accompany his wife into the delivery room, and he helped in the best way he could, by holding his wife's hand and encouraging her throughout her labour. He looked so proud and happy when Abigail laid the newly-born baby boy in his arms.

She was walking down the corridor on her way out of the hospital when she almost bumped into Marc. He grasped her by the shoulders.

'What are you doing here?'

She smiled wearily up at him. 'Would you believe, delivering a baby?'

'I suppose it hasn't slipped your mind that you're marrying me tomorrow?' he asked wryly.

She clicked her fingers. 'Of course—that's it! I knew there was something I had to do tomorrow!'

But he didn't share the joke. 'I'm sure if you'd asked, someone would have filled in for you today—Sister Gregson, perhaps.'

'Sister Gregson is on holiday until Monday,' she told him. 'Besides, I can't just drop patients like that. Some, I'll have to of course, but I wanted to make sure they were all right as far as I could and didn't feel they were being passed around like parcels!' She looked up at him. 'Surely you can understand that?'

He slipped an arm round her waist. 'All right. There's no need to go all defensive. I just thought you'd have a lot to do, and I don't want my bride tiring herself out.' He grinned at her. 'I could take a ten-minute break— what about a quick cup of tea?'

She shook her head, glancing at her watch. 'Sorry. There was a message for me as I was leaving the GP

Unit. I'm wanted in the SNO's office before I leave. Then I still have another couple of calls to make before I finally put up the shutters.' Even as she said the words, a little wave of nostalgia washed over her and she swallowed hard. Marc squeezed her waist.

'Oh yes, I'd almost forgotten about that. I expect you've guessed that they want to give you a bit of a send-off. I'm warning you in case you find it all a bit emotional.' He bent to kiss her briefly. 'See you tomorrow then, darling.' His eyes searched hers. 'You won't keep me waiting too long, will you?'

She smiled softly. 'No—I won't.'

He had been right; all her friends were waiting for her in the Senior Nursing Officer's office. There was a bottle of champagne, plates of canapés and, on Maureen Russell's desk, a pile of prettily-wrapped presents. Marc had also been right in his assumption that it would be an emotional occasion. For the first few moments Abigail's throat was tight and she had difficulty in keeping the tears back. When she was toasted and there were cries of 'Speech!', Joan Marshall came to her rescue.

'I think I can speak for all of us here when I say that Abigail will be a great loss to the GP Unit and to the mums-to-be of Rinkley in general,' she said. 'But here's wishing her every happiness—and as many babies of her own as she wants to deliver!'

There was laughter all round and the moment of tension passed. Abigail took a sip of her champagne and smiled at the faces of her friends. 'Thank you all—for the party and for the lovely presents. I hope I shall be delivering more of other people's babies for a while, before I make a start on my own collection, but thanks, Joan, for the thought!'

Amid the general chatter afterwards Joan came up to

her. 'I haven't had the chance to congratulate you properly yet.' She looked at Abigail shrewdly. 'You know, you're a bit of a dark horse; the last time I spoke to you, you pretended that you and Marc weren't seeing each other any more—next thing we hear is that you're engaged!' Embarrassed, Abigail muttered something incoherent into her glass and Joan went on, 'I didn't know you were intending to carry on nursing after your marriage.'

'I hope to.' Abigail was glad to change the subject. 'Marc doesn't seem too keen, but I'm quite determined. I'd be bored to death just sitting around at home all day.'

Joan drew the corners of her mouth down doubtfully. 'From what I hear about the family home, it will take some running. You may find you've more to do than sit around, even if you don't get a job.' She filled Abigail's glass. 'Are any of his family coming over for the wedding?'

Abigail shook her head. 'No. There are only the two of them now, his uncle and cousin—both doctors in the family practice, so they won't be able to leave. Marc says they'll be giving a party for us over there later.'

'So neither of you will have any relatives there? What a pity.' Joan took a sip from her glass, then smiled at Abigail over its rim. 'Mind you, it could have its compensations. When I was married two of my aunts decided to have the row of all time! It almost ruined the day. There's often a lot to be said for a quiet wedding!'

When Abigail got home that evening she closed the door and looked round. All day she had been acutely aware of doing things for the last time. The hall was crowded with boxes packed with her belongings, waiting to be picked up tomorrow. They would follow her to Guernsey later. Her going-away case containing her trousseau was already at Helen's where she would be going herself first thing in the morning. Joan Marshall had offered to come home with her and spend the night but she had refused. Now she regretted the decision. It would have been comforting to have another woman to chat to, she told herself firmly, pushing aside the thought that Joan would have stopped her thinking—panicking about whether or not she was making a mistake, marrying Marc in so much haste.

It was the perfect morning for a wedding—sun shining in a clear blue sky, birds singing and everything looking fresh and new. Abigail woke at dawn and found herself quite unable to go to sleep again so, as soon as she decently could, she got up, showered and dressed and drove over to the Curtis's house in the little car that after today would no longer be hers.

She found Helen in the kitchen, still wearing her dressing-gown. She looked up in surprise when Abigail tapped on the window.

'Heavens! You're early.' She opened the back door to let her in. 'I know just how you feel though. I didn't sleep a wink on the night before my wedding.' She took the case out of Abigail's hand. 'You know, by rights you should be having a lie-in and your breakfast in bed. I had the guest room all ready for you to change in and so on, then Marc's aunt arrived unexpectedly last night and I had to put her in there.'

Abigail frowned. 'His aunt—what aunt is that? I thought there was only his Uncle Simon and his cousin Leslie.'

'Apparently this is a distant relative by marriage—a cousin of his mother's or something. It seems she was visiting an old schoolfriend in England and "felt it her duty to represent the family".' Helen smiled as she poured Abigail a large cup of coffee. 'She's a funny old thing, but quite sweet. And it's nice that there'll be one relative at least at the wedding, isn't it?'

Abigail sat down at the table. 'I'm sorry, Helen. It must have put you out, having her descend on you like that.'

'Not at all,' Helen smiled. 'I got the boys to double up and made Peter clear out his room so that you could use that. It was long overdue for a clear-out anyway, so it was a good excuse to make him do it.' She bustled about the kitchen, getting eggs and bacon out of the fridge. 'Now—you're going to have a good breakfast whether you want it or not. If I know anything about weddings, you won't get much to eat for the rest of the day. After that we'd better see if your dress needs pressing.'

Wedding fever seemed to have taken hold of the Curtis household and, from behind her closed door, Abigail could hear Helen organising her husband and two sons relentlessly. As she stood before the mirror in the small, masculine room that belonged to Peter Curtis, Abigail felt oddly detached—as though she were a casual observer instead of one of the main protagonists, the *bride*. She said the word quietly to herself, but it seemed to mean nothing. She simply couldn't identify with it. Did everyone feel like this, she wondered? Was it because she had no one of her own here? Was it the haste with which she had been precipitated into it all? It certainly wasn't that she didn't love Marc; the mere thought of him was enough to set her pulses racing. If only her father were here, she thought sadly. She could have talked to him as to no one else; confessed all her fears as she had done so many times over the years. He had always had the knack of putting the worst of her doubts into perspective for her.

A tap on the door brought her out of her reverie with a start and she opened it to find Helen outside with a small dumpy woman in tow. Helen looked at her in surprise.

'Still not dressed? You'd better hurry if you're to be at the church on time. I thought that before we left you should meet Marc's Aunt Honoria.'

The other woman stepped forward, smiling. She wore a brilliantly coloured floral dress, and a white straw hat with a bunch of nodding daisies was perched rakishly on top of her tightly permed grey hair. She beamed at Abigail through gold-framed spectacles and held out her hand.

'My dear, I am so pleased to meet dear Marcus's future wife. I hope you'll both be very happy.'

'Thank you.' Abigail shook the plump hand. 'It was very good of you to come.'

Helen looked at her watch and pushed her back into the room. 'Do get dressed now, dear. Aunt Honoria and I are off to the church with Peter and Andrew. Bill is waiting for you downstairs—so nervous you'd think he was getting married himself! I saw Marc and his best man leave about ten minutes ago. Is there anything you need help with before I go?'

Abigail shook her head. 'No, I have only to slip the dress on and I'm ready.'

'Sure? No awkward zips or anything?'

'No—really, I'm fine.'

'That's all right then. Good luck, dear—see you in church.'

When Abigail came downstairs, Bill Curtis was waiting for her. He got to his feet and held out both his hands.

'My dear girl, you look enchanting. Marc is a very lucky fellow.' He glanced at his watch. 'We still have a minute. Can I get you something—a brandy? Steady your nerves.'

She shook her head and he laughed. 'Well, I expect you're wise. Don't want to breathe alcohol over the vicar, eh? Hardly the right image!'

Abigail stole a look at herself in the hall mirror. Even now that she was dressed, she still didn't feel like a bride. It was strange—almost as though it was all happening to someone else.

The church was cool and fragrant with the scent of flowers. It was surprisingly full. It seemed that she and Marc had more friends than she had thought. Bill smiled reassuringly at her as they waited in the porch, then the organ struck up the first chords of the wedding march and they were walking down the aisle, Abigail's eyes on Marc's tall, straight figure. And then she was beside him. He turned to smile down at her and suddenly everything came into focus. It *was* real—it *was* happening. She smiled back at him and the vicar stepped forward to begin the ceremony.

They emerged into the sunlight—then there were photographs, confetti, kisses and good wishes. Some of the nurses from the Wellbourne had managed to get along and a good many of the patients. Some were standing outside the church gates with the babies Abigail had recently delivered, waiting to get a glimpse and throw a handful of confetti. At last she and Marc were in the car and on their way back to the Curtis's house. Marc turned to her with a sigh.

'Well, that's all over!' He drew her close and kissed her. 'And how does it feel to be Mrs DeLisle?'

She laughed and relaxed against him. 'Wonderful. Somehow none of it seemed real until I came into the church and saw you standing there. I'm glad it's over.'

He looked at her quizzically. 'Was it such an ordeal? You look quite beautiful, do you know that?'

Suddenly, as his eyes devoured her, she felt shy. 'It was odd, your aunt turning up like that,' she said. His face clouded.

'More than odd—it was a cheek, arriving out of the blue like that, uninvited! She isn't an aunt either, just married to some distant cousin of my mother's. She's an interfering old busybody—out for a bit of free entertainment. I was furious when she descended on Helen last night, but Helen was so nice about it there was nothing I could do.'

Abigail looked at him in surprise. 'I thought she seemed quite sweet, the little I saw of her.'

'I just hope she doesn't let me down by having too much to drink,' Marc said, his lips tightly compressed.

'She's not an alcoholic, is she? Abigail asked in alarm.

Marc laughed and squeezed her hand. 'No—nothing so dramatic. It's just that she tends to get rather garrulous when she's had a couple of sherries. It could be embarrassing.' He pulled her arm through his. 'Never mind her—a few more hours and we'll be on the plane for Guernsey, just the two of us. I can hardly wait!'

The Curtis's lounge was decked with flowers and the french windows were open so that the guests could overflow into the garden. The buffet lunch that Helen had laid on was sumptuous; temptingly set out on a long table at one end of the room, the centre-piece being the gleaming white three-tiered wedding cake. Champagne corks popped and speeches were made. Hand in hand, Marc and Abigail circulated, chatting to the guests, expressing thanks for presents and exchanging small talk. They were talking to Marc's best man, one of the younger doctors in the group practice, when Helen touched Abigail's arm.

'I'm sorry to bother you, dear, but I'm a little concerned about Marc's aunt. She's sitting over there all by herself and she seems so out of things. I've tried introducing her to people but it doesn't seem to be doing any good. Would you go over and have a word with her?'

'Of course.'

Abigail went over to where the old lady was sitting. The way Helen had described her behaviour didn't fit in at all with what Marc had said in the car. Perhaps Aunt Honoria wasn't feeling well. She slipped into the chair beside her and touched her arm.

'Are you all right—er—Auntie?' she asked. 'Are you enjoying yourself? Can I get you anything?' She reached out to take the empty glass and plate from the old lady's hand. Aunt Honoria turned to look at her, her expression glassy.

'Oh dear—I've let you down, my dear. I came here with the best of intentions, but now I'm too late!'

Abigail frowned. What was she talking about? Had she already had too much to drink? She leaned forward. 'How do you mean—it's too late?'

Aunt Honoria peered at her, seeming to see her clearly for the first time. 'I should have made it my business to tell you!' She grasped Abigail's arm. 'He's marrying you for the money—you know that, don't you?'

Abigail laughed. Obviously she *had* had too much to drink. 'That's absurd. I haven't got any money.' She took the old woman's arm. 'Let me take you upstairs for a nice lie down. I'm sure you'll feel better for it.'

As they crossed the room she looked around for Marc, but she couldn't see him anywhere. Helen looked busy too, but she caught Abigail's eye and nodded her understanding of what was going on. On the landing Abigail paused outside the guest room, then opened the door and propelled the old lady firmly inside. 'Would you like to lie on the bed? Shall I help you with your shoes?' she asked, but the old lady shook her head.

'I'll just have a quiet sit down, then I'll be all right.'

'And you're sure you don't want anything?' Abigail asked from the door.

'Sit down and talk to me for a minute.'

Abigail hesitated, thinking of Marc and the guests, but she didn't like leaving the old lady in case she wandered out on to the landing and fell down the stairs. Reluctantly she sat on the edge of a chair.

'Well—just for a minute then.'

Aunt Honoria sighed. 'You seem such a nice girl, so considerate,' she mumbled. 'I hope he realises how lucky he is—those DeLisles—so arrogant, so proud.' She seemed to be wandering again, then suddenly she looked sharply at Abigail and said, 'Didn't you ever wonder why he wanted to get married in such a hurry?'

A feeling of uneasiness began to stir in the pit of Abigail's stomach. 'I—don't know what you mean,' she said haltingly. 'His father died, that was the reason—' She broke off as the old woman shook her head knowingly.

'And the will—did he tell you about that?'

Abigail shook her head. 'No, I don't know—' She stood up and began to back towards the door, afraid of what she was about to hear. 'I don't think you should—'

'Marcus was only to benefit from his father's will if he was married at the time of his death!' The old lady stared at her. 'At the time, or within three months of it. So now you know!'

Abigail felt the blood drain from her cheeks. Surely there must be some mistake? Marc would never do that to her—would never use her in such a shameful way. She forced a laugh. 'What a strange condition to make,' she said lightly. 'Whatever justification could Marc's father have had for that?'

'Plenty!' Aunt Honoria leaned forward, warming to her subject. 'The main one being that Marcus is the last male member of the DeLisle family and his father was desperately keen for him to have an heir. But there are other reasons too,' she added darkly. 'Marcus was always flitting from flower to flower as the saying goes—too fond of the girls for his father's liking. That would never do for a family doctor. Then there was the business with that cousin!'

Abigail looked up. 'Cousin? Do you mean his Cousin Leslie?'

The old lady nodded. 'Very close they were—always together as children and when they were growing up. Then when she broke off her engagement and came back to Guernsey to work in the practice—'

'Just a minute!' Abigail's head was spinning. 'Do you mean that his cousin is a *girl*?' But the old lady was well into her stride now and there was no stopping her.

'Stephen—Marcus's father—was always afraid that they might marry one day—dead against that, he was. That was another clause in the will—Marcus was to get nothing at all if he formed an alliance with Lesley DeLisle. That shows you how strongly he felt!' As though getting the weight of all this off her chest had suddenly exhausted her, the old lady lay back on the bed and closed her eyes. 'Oh dear—I'm quite tired after all. I think I will have that little sleep. It's such a relief to have done my duty and told you what you have a right to know.'

Almost instantly she was asleep, and as Abigail closed the door softly behind her she could hear the old lady's gentle snores. She was standing at the top of the stairs, deep in troubled thought, when Helen Curtis started up from the bottom. Looking up, she caught sight of Abigail.

'I was just coming to rescue you—' She broke off. 'My dear, you're as white as a ghost! Is anything the matter?'

Abigail shook her head. How could she tell Helen what Marc's aunt had just revealed to her? How could she tell *anyone*? She tried to smile.

'It's just the excitement,' she said. 'And the fact that I had hardly any sleep last night.'

Helen slipped an arm round her waist. 'You'll be just fine once you and Marc are on that plane. He's been looking everywhere for you. It's time for you to change now. Come along.'

In the impersonal little bedroom Abigail changed into the hyacinth blue linen suit she was to wear for the journey. Leaning forward, she peered into the mirror, looking critically at the face that stared back at her. So Marc was marrying her on the rebound—marrying her because the girl he really loved was denied to him. Why couldn't she have realised that it couldn't be for herself he wanted her? She felt she had never looked more plain with her straight, mousy hair and her ordinary, run-of-the-mill looks. If Lesley DeLisle had the family looks she would be a beauty, and Abigail didn't doubt that she was. How could she have fooled herself into thinking that Marc would choose a girl like her without good reason? In a sudden panic she realised just how little she knew about the man she had married—how little about his family and his background. What was it Aunt Honoria had said? 'Those DeLisles—so arrogant, so proud!'

CHAPTER FOUR

'DARLING, wake up. We're almost there.' Marc gently shook Abigail's arm. 'I don't want you to miss your first glimpse of my island—your new home!'

Abigail hadn't been asleep, only pretending. Almost as soon as they had boarded the plane she had closed her eyes and feigned sleep, afraid of speaking to Marc—of looking into those golden eyes and capitulating before she had had time to think out what to do. There must be something in what Aunt Honoria had told her, otherwise she surely would not have dared to say such things. Could she have misinterpreted the vital clause in the will—perhaps heard some garbled version? She really should speak to Marc about it as soon as she could; get the whole thing out in the open and cleared up. If only she could bring herself to broach the subject. Deep inside—so deep that she wouldn't even admit it to herself—she was terribly afraid that it was all too true.

She opened her eyes and looked at him. He smiled, making her heart twist inside her.

'Are you feeling rested? You've had a good sleep.' He leaned across her to point as the plane began to lose height. 'There—look.'

Abigail gasped as she looked down. There, in a smooth, blue sea, the island of Guernsey sparkled like a jewel—a diamond, its facets glittering in the brilliance of the setting sun. 'Oh!' she breathed. 'Oh—it's beautiful. What makes it sparkle so?'

'The glasshouses,' Marc explained. 'It's a horticultural island, don't forget.'

Abigail watched, fascinated, as the plane dipped nearer. After the rocky coast came a patchwork of fields in every shade of green from emerald to russet, divided by blue-green hedges and dotted here and there with the red of house roofs. Again, here and there like scattered sequins, glasshouses flashed in the evening sunshine. Impulsively, her hand reached for Marc's.

'I'd no idea it was so lovely.' She turned to look into his eyes. 'Where is King's Rock?'

He leaned across her once more to point. 'On the south side of the island. It looks minute from up here. I think it's the most beautiful bay in the whole of the bailiwick, but then I might just be prejudiced.' He smiled and squeezed her hand, and she caught a little of his infectious excitement. He really did love this place. She looked at his face and a dull ache began deep inside her. Why couldn't it have been as perfect as she had wanted it to be? If only Aunt Honoria hadn't come to the wedding. If only she didn't know about that hateful clause in Marc's father's will!

At the airport the hired car that Marc had ordered was waiting. As they drove along the narrow, leafy lanes Marc pointed out all the places of interest with obvious delight. At last the car turned in through tall wrought-iron gates and he turned to her.

'This is it—your new home, Mrs DeLisle.'

Abigail looked around her in wonder. It seemed that the rumours Joan Marshall had heard were not exaggerated. At the end of a long, azalea-lined drive they came out of the cool shadows on to a broad sweep of gravel, in the centre of which was a circular lawn, dominated by a huge old cedar tree. But it was the house itself that made

Abigail catch her breath. Built of pearly-grey stone it stood, square and solid, its slate roof lavender-coloured in the mellow evening light. The ground floor windows were long, and squarely in the centre was the white-painted front door, standing invitingly open. The car drew up to it and Abigail got out, breathing in the clear air with its faint salty tang. Marc and the driver busied themselves with the luggage, carrying the cases in through the open door while Abigail stood gazing about her. Then, with a call and a revving of the engine, the car was disappearing down the drive. Marc touched her arm. They were alone.

'I believe this is where I carry you over the threshold.' He was looking down at her, his eyes teasing. Suddenly wild panic filled her chest and throat. She wanted to run away.

'No, please—your housekeeper . . . I'd feel so silly.'

'She isn't here,' he told her calmly. 'She has her own cottage, not far away. I spoke to her last night on the telephone. She said she'd leave a cold meal for us and make herself scarce. She's a very tactful woman, Mrs Morelle.' Laughing at her protests, he swung her up into his arms. 'So you see, darling, you don't really have any choice. All the DeLisle brides get carried over this threshold and it would be bad luck to break the tradition.' He set her down gently in the cool, shadowy hall with its flagged floor. Abigail began to turn away but he caught her to him and held her close, looking down into her eyes.

'Well—what do you think? I'd like to hear your first impressions.'

She looked round at the oak-panelled walls and antique furniture, rich with the patina of years of polishing. Close to the door a huge bowl of early roses stood on a low chest, filling the hall with heady fragrance.

'It's—lovely,' Abigail said haltingly. 'If a little over-whelming.'

He looked at her for a long moment. 'I do believe you're shy suddenly!' He lifted her chin with one finger to look into her eyes. 'There's nothing wrong, is there? You were very quiet on the plane. Aren't you feeling well?'

She shook her head. 'I'm fine—a little tired, maybe.'

Bending his head, he brushed her lips with his and at once she felt her senses stir. What did it matter—all that business about the will?—she asked herself fiercely. She would *make* Marc glad that he had married her—that was the only thing to concentrate on now. She melted into his arms, her body moulding itself to his as she responded to his kiss with all the desire that flared up within her. He released her and looked down into her eyes.

'I don't believe you've had anything to eat since breakfast. Shall we see what Mrs Morelle has left for us?'

She bit her lip, wanting to go on kissing him, to stay in his arms until she had convinced herself that she had been right to marry him and come to this fairy-tale place. She opened her mouth to tell him so, but instead heard herself saying, 'Yes, if you like.'

He picked up her hand and tucked it into the crook of his arm. 'Afterwards you shall have a guided tour of the house and hear its history.'

The supper left out for them by Mrs Morelle was delicious; a seafood salad with fruit and cream to follow. Marc opened the fridge and took out a bottle of wine that had been chilling inside. After two glasses Abigail felt more relaxed.

They left the dishes in the sink and Marc held out his

hand to her. 'On second thoughts, perhaps we'll leave the ground floor rooms till the morning.' He smiled. 'For tonight the rooms on the first floor are all you need to see, I think.' He was teasing her again. Just a few days ago she would have risen to the challenge, countering with a witty remark of her own, enjoying the gentle game of verbal sparring. Now she was tongue-tied, acutely embarrassed as she followed him up the wide staircase, her hand firmly held in his.

At the top of the stairs hung a large portrait of a handsome man dressed in the clothes of the Restoration period. Marc paused before it.

'That is Pierre DeLisle, the wicked ancestor I told you about.'

Abigail studied the striking face with its satanic black beard and dark glittering eyes. 'He doesn't look much like you,' she remarked. 'Did he build this house?'

He shook his head. 'Not this one. The one he built was burned down in the latter part of the eighteenth century, but this one was raised on the same spot. It was Pierre who started the tradition of carrying the bride across the threshold.'

'He doesn't look the romantic sort to me,' Abigail said, looking at the portrait, her head on one side. Marc laughed.

'He wasn't! *His* bride came over the threshold kicking and screaming. He'd abducted her, you see. She was a beautiful island girl whose father had refused Pierre her hand.'

'So he took it instead?'

'And the rest of her with it!' Marc shook his head. 'That's one trait he handed down. We still don't accept refusal lightly—though I hope we're more civilised about it today.' They walked down a short corridor and Marc pushed open a door at the end of it. Stepping through, he drew her inside. 'Tell me what you think.'

She was acutely aware of the door closing behind her as she looked around the spacious, airy room. The walls were panelled in a silky pale wood and the space seemed dominated by a huge four-poster bed. Clearly the room had been refurbished. Fresh white frilled curtains billowed gently at the long windows and the bed and skirted dressing-table were flounced to match. Marc looked at her.

'Do you like it? There's a view of the sea from the window.'

Abigail moistened her lips. 'It's—beautiful.'

'There's a bathroom through there.' He pointed to a door, pulling off his jacket and tie. 'Would you like to take a shower while I bring up the rest of the cases?' He looked at her, his thick brows coming together, intensifying the crease between them. 'Abby—what's the matter? There is something, isn't there? You haven't been yourself ever since we left England.' He crossed the room and grasped her shoulders, looking down at her—feeling her trembling vibrating through his fingers. 'You're not—*afraid* of me, are you?'

She shook her head. 'Of course I'm not.'

'Then what?'

She raised her eyes to his, teeth catching at her lower lip. Should she tell him now that she knew about the clause in the will, his reason for marrying her, his love for his cousin? But before she could begin to frame the words, his lips were on hers, kissing her gently, persuasively—sliding her jacket from her shoulders and down her arms. She made a feeble attempt to stop him, then told herself weakly that he had the right. He was her husband—this was their wedding night.

Gently, but with deliberation, he removed the lacy blouse and the wisp of bra she wore beneath it, and a shiver of ecstasy went through her as he bent to press his lips into the hollow of her throat. As he released the fastening of her skirt his hands traced the line of her ribs till they cupped the small breasts.

'I told you it would be perfect,' he whispered, his mouth against hers. His hands were cool on her naked back as he drew her against him. 'Here at King's Rock in our own room.' He lifted her gently, putting her down in the centre of the huge bed and a moment later he lay beside her. Her pulses raced as she felt his flesh against hers, the feather-softness of his caresses. The room was dim and quiet and the only sound was of their breathing, but Abigail was sure that he must hear the beating of her heart as his caresses grew more urgent. Trembling, she closed her arms around him, trying desperately to shut out the doubts that tormented her. Once she belonged to him everything would be all right, she told herself. It was really so simple.

She found his mouth and tried to tell him with her kiss that she loved and needed him. Her hands moved caressingly over the strong muscles of his back and she arched her body towards him—then suddenly Aunt Honoria's voice rose, unbidden in her mind. 'Marcus was to get nothing at all if he formed an alliance with Lesley DeLisle—that shows you how strongly he felt about it!' The girl had broken off her engagement to return to Guernsey—was that because the bond between her and Marc was so strong? Like a pricked bubble, Abigail's desire faded. The tension left her body and she opened her eyes to stare up at him.

'Marc, I'm sorry—I can't.'

For a moment he lay poised above her, then he rolled away from her with a moan, jaw clenched and eyes tightly shut. For a moment there was silence, then he turned to her and smiled.

'It's all right. Don't worry. There's plenty of time.' He raised himself on one elbow to look down at her, stroking the heavy fringe of hair back from her forehead. 'There is something wrong, isn't there? Can't you tell me what it is?'

She closed her eyes and sighed deeply. Her whole body felt leaden with misery. She longed to tell him and have her fears laughed away, to have the intolerable burden of suspicion lifted from her so that she could love him as she longed to. She turned her head to look directly into his eyes.

'Marc, why didn't you tell me that your cousin Lesley was a girl?'

His eyes widened in surprise. 'Didn't I? I suppose I just assumed that you knew.'

'It *is* a man's name too,' she reminded him.

'I suppose it is—I never thought.' He frowned. 'What does this have to do with anything?'

She sat up and turned away, unable to meet his eyes. 'It's just one of a lot of things you haven't told me.' She bit her lip. 'Can you tell me why you asked me to marry you, Marc? Can you tell me *truthfully*, I mean?'

He sat up and grasped her shoulders, turning her to face him, his eyes narrowing darkly. 'What *is* all this? I think you'd better tell me, don't you?'

Acutely aware of her nakedness, she pulled herself from him, turning her back until she had drawn on the bathrobe that lay over the arm of a chair by the bed. She turned to him, tying the belt.

'Tell me about your father's will—about a certain special clause in it.'

He shook his head. 'I don't know what you're talking about.'

'Of *course* you do!' Her voice rose shrilly. Now that she had said the words—now that it was out in the open—the relief was enormous. But for him to try to deny it!

'At least be honest about it, Marc,' she threw at him. 'I know now that this is simply a marriage of convenience. If I'd known at the time you asked me to marry you I would have refused. As it is, we're married now and there's nothing to be done about it, but you might at least try not to insult my intelligence by protesting your innocence!'

He sprang up from the bed and faced her angrily. 'Who has been talking to you? Was it that old witch, Honoria? What on earth has she been saying?'

'Nothing I wasn't entitled to know,' Abigail retorted. 'She simply told me about the clause in your father's will. In order to benefit, you had to be married within three months of his death!'

There was a silence as they stared at each other. Abigail was aware of the gentle swish the curtains made as they moved against the sill, and for the first time she could just hear the distant roar of the sea. Marc's face drained of colour as he stood looking at her. In the few moments it had taken her to tell him what she knew, he had altered; suddenly she saw with a small shock that he did, after all, resemble his ancestor, Pierre. His eyes had darkened, glittering dangerously, and the golden skin had become grey, a white rim outlining his mouth. His fists clenched and unclenched at his sides and his chest rose and fell ominously. She took a step backwards, alarmed at the intensity of his fury, but his hands shot out to grab her shoulders. He jerked her to him, looking down menacingly.

'And you believed all this?' he demanded in a low growl. 'You believed it all—without question?'

She looked up at him defiantly, her heart beating fast. 'Are you going to deny it?'

His fingers sank into her flesh until she winced with pain. She could feel him trembling with rage. 'My *God*! I should—' He looked down at her, nostrils flaring. 'We're married now—you're my wife. I don't have to admit or deny anything! How *dare* you accuse me?'

She cried out as he pulled the bathrobe from her roughly, revealing her creamy shoulders and breasts. Tugging at the fastening, he tore it from her and tossed it into a corner of the room, then he lifted her and threw her on to the bed. She retreated to the farthest side and curled herself into a defensive ball, warding him off with outstretched hands.

'If you touch me I'll—I'll—' He checked, taking a step backwards, then picking up his shirt from a chair he began to dress rapidly.

'All right, Abby—you have it your way,' he said tightly, his back towards her. 'A marriage of convenience, you called it. Well, if you've made up your mind, then that is what you shall have!' Swiftly he knotted his tie and drew on his jacket. Then, raking a hand through his dishevelled hair, he strode out of the room without a backward glance, slamming the door behind him.

Still hunched in her corner of the bed, she heard his retreating feet and then, somewhere in the distance, the thud of the front door. She listened tensely, teeth so tightly clamped on her lower lip that she tasted blood on her tongue. A few moments later she heard the roar of an engine and the crunch of wheels on gravel—then silence.

Slowly she uncoiled and lay face downward on the rumpled sheets, burying her face into the pillow as the first sobs tore from her throat. It was all spoilt—her marriage to Marc was over before it had begun. Why couldn't she have kept her knowledge to herself? She could have worked at it, made Marc love her as much as she loved him, if only it hadn't been for her stupid pride. Now it was too late—in a few short minutes she had killed whatever he might have felt for her stone dead!

CHAPTER FIVE

SHE WOKE early and lay quite still in the big, empty bed,
trying to separate reality from the disturbed dreams that
had invaded her sleep. Above her the muslin frills of the
bed's canopy fluttered slightly in the morning breeze
blowing in through the open window. She moaned softly
as the events of the previous night drifted slowly back
into her consciousness.

She had lain awake for what felt like hours, her ears
straining for the sound of a car returning—racking her
brain to think what she should do. Eventually her mind,
exhausted with the effort of trying to solve the problem,
had simply switched off and she had fallen into a restless
sleep through which the dreams had writhed and twisted
like poisonous snakes. She was going through her wedding again, smiling happily up at Marc—walking hand in
hand with him through the house. Then suddenly he had
gone, and in his place stood the sinister Pierre, dark
glittering eyes laughing, hands reaching out for her as
she fled, screaming, down endless corridors. She sighed
and stretched her stiff limbs. The reality seemed little
better than the dreams. There was no awakening from
that!

Abigail swung her legs over the edge of the bed and
pulled on her bathrobe, picking it up from the floor
where Marc had thrown it. Going over to the window,
she leaned out, breathing the fresh, sparkling air
gratefully. Even through her misery she could not help
but catch her breath in wonder at the beauty of the vista

spread below her. This room was at the back of the
house and looked over a garden that sloped away towards the cliff's edge. Clipped lawns gave way to cluster-
ing trees and beyond, in the distance, was the turquoise
sparkle of the sea and the curved line of the coast, lazy in
the morning mist. Mingled with the early chorus of birds
came the soft murmur of the sea and the call of gulls.
What a perfect morning it would have been to begin
their married life, if only . . . She turned away from the
window, the beauty suddenly too painful to look at.

In the pretty bathroom with its cool lemon tiles she
showered and dressed in a simple blue cotton dress,
running a comb through her hair. The face that looked
back at her from the mirror was pale and hollow-eyed,
but she made no attempt to improve it with make-up.
Where was Marc, she wondered? Where had he gone
last night? To Lesley, perhaps. Had he returned at all?
One thing was certain, in a moment she must open the
door, leave the security of this room and go downstairs
to face whatever the day would bring. She got up from
the dressing-table and took a deep breath, opening the
door and stepping out on to the landing.

The house was silent. It was early, not yet six o'clock.
She wondered what time Mrs Morelle, the housekeeper,
started work. The old staircase creaked gently under her
feet as she went downstairs. At the foot she paused. At
least she knew where the kitchen was—she could make
herself a cup of tea.

It was a beautiful kitchen, large and airy, the perfect
mixture of old and new. Under the window that faced on
to a walled courtyard there was a stainless steel sink,
spotless and gleaming, while on the other side of the
room an old pine dresser filled one wall, its shelves
ranged with copper pans and blue and white china.

Abigail could imagine the huge Aga in its recess giving off a welcoming warmth on winter days, but she had already noticed a discreetly built-in oven and hob that ran on electricity. She filled the kettle and switched it on, taking milk from the fridge, a cup and saucer from the dresser—then she turned and her hand flew to her throat as she saw Marc standing in the doorway silently watching her.

'Oh! You startled me—I thought—' She dropped the cup she had been holding and it fell to the floor with a crash, splintering into a dozen pieces. With a cry she bent to pick them up. Marc did not move from where he stood in the doorway.

'We have to talk, Abigail—before the day starts properly. There's a lot to sort out.'

She looked up at him, noticing for the first time that he wore different clothes to last night and that he was freshly shaved. He had returned then? His voice sounded tight, yet he had said they must talk. A flicker of impatience crossed his brow as she fumbled with the broken china.

'For God's sake leave that!' he snapped. 'Mrs Morelle will see to it when she comes in. Come into the study. I refuse to discuss our future over the kitchen sink!'

She followed him quietly into the study, a small square room leading off the hall. Three of the walls were lined with books and under the window stood a large oak desk. He pointed to a chair, but she didn't sit down. He towered over her enough as it was. She didn't want to feel completely dominated by his height and his masculinity. He looked at her for a moment.

'First, I owe you an apology,' he said. 'I lost my temper last night. I almost—well, anyway—I'm sorry.'

She moistened her dry lips. 'Perhaps it's I who

should—' He cut off her words with an impatient wave of his hand.

'No post-mortems, please. I've apologised. Let it stand at that.' He sat down at his desk and, after a moment's hesitation, she followed, sitting in the chair he had indicated. He picked up a pencil and rolled it between his fingers reflectively.

'I have a proposal to make.' He looked up at her. 'You are, no doubt, eager to get away from here as soon as you can; to forget all about me and this—unfortunate mess you find yourself in.' She stared at him, unable to assess his mood. His voice was cool and level and yet . . . She opened her mouth to speak, but he continued. 'But I'm afraid I can't allow that, Abigail. I don't take kindly to being made to look a fool, especially by a woman.'

She half rose. 'Surely I am the one who has been made to look foolish!'

He appeared not to have heard. 'I am about to make a bargain with you. Will you agree to stay on here for one year and to put on a show of normality publicly? After that time is up you will be free to do as you like.'

Abigail sat down again and looked at him. Obviously he was making this request because of the terms of his father's will. She was to stay here in this impossible situation—pretending to the outside world that their marriage was perfect—just so that those terms could be met.

'When the divorce goes through I shall see to it that you receive a generous allowance, of course, and while you are here I shall do my best to make sure you are as comfortable as possible under the circumstances,' he said quickly.

Abigail stared at him coldly. 'We're not *all* so preoccupied with money and comfort,' she said cuttingly. She was rewarded by the dull flush that coloured his face, but he made no countering reply.

'Well, what is your answer? He looked up. 'Perhaps you would like time to consider?' The tone of his voice was cool, but when he looked up at her his eyes flashed briefly, reminding her of the scene last night.

Confused thoughts chased themselves through Abigail's brain. It would all be so neat. He had married her and satisfied his father's whim. After a year there would be a quick divorce and he could marry Lesley and—presumably—live happily ever after. But what was to become of her? Where would *she* go and what would she do with the rest of her ruined life? It seemed he cared less now than when he had chosen her to be a pawn in his cruel game.

Bitter resentment made her voice sharp as she said, 'Perhaps you're forgetting that I'm a nurse and not an actress! What makes you so confident that I'd be able to keep up this—this charade?'

He looked at her calmly. 'You don't seem to have had any trouble in showing your feelings for me in the past—and it will not be without effort on my part too, remember.'

Quick tears sprang to her eyes as the cruel barb found its mark. She rose to her feet hurriedly and went towards the door. 'I want to leave here now, today.'

He jumped up to grasp her arm. 'No, Abby—don't do that. Please think about my suggestion. You won't regret it, I promise. I believe—I believe we owe it to each other to do as I say.'

She stared up at him, acutely aware of his hand on her bare arm. His touch still had the power to make her pulses race. Her resolve weakened. How could she go back to Rinkley on the day following her wedding? What

would she say to all the people who had been so kind?
The prospect was out of the question. Yet where else
could she go? If she left here now the marriage would be
declared null and void. Marc would not then get his
inheritance. His motive in asking her to stay was crystal
clear, so why shouldn't she use it for her own convenience, stay here until she could think of an alternative? He had used her, so why shouldn't she use
him?

His hand dropped to his side, but he went on looking
at her. 'Well?'

She lifted her chin. 'I'll stay on one condition. I want
to work—to nurse.'

He looked relieved. 'As you please. I'm sure we can
sort something out.' He paused, glancing at her. 'Thank
you. I promise you that I shall make no demands beyond
those you find reasonable.'

She bit back the retort that the whole idea was unreasonable. It would do no good to row about it. If they
were to live under the same roof for the coming year and
put on a show of married bliss to the world at large, they
would have to learn to be indifferent, unemotional—
otherwise it would be intolerable. 'Thank you. I appreciate that,' she said bleakly.

The sound of a door shutting made them both look up.
'That will be Mrs Morelle. You'd better come and meet
her.' Marc took her arm, but she stiffened and shrank
from him. He sighed and looked at her.

'Please, Abigail. We have to make a start somewhere.
It might as well be here and now.'

They found the housekeeper in the kitchen, on her
knees with a dustpan and brush clearing up the broken
china. When she saw them she got to her feet hurriedly,
and Abigail saw that she was a tall, well-built woman

with a halo of white curls and a gentle smile. She put down her dustpan and held out her hands.

'Dr Marcus! How lovely to see you. I hope everything was all right for you last night—the supper and your room.'

Marc took her hands and kissed her on both cheeks. 'Everything was fine. It's lovely to see you too, Morrie. Sorry about the cup. I'm afraid it was my fault. May I present my wife?' He stood aside. Abigail held out her hand and the housekeeper took it, smiling warmly.

'Congratulations. It'll be so nice to have a mistress at DeLisle House again after all these years. May I wish you good luck and welcome to our island, madam?'

Abigail smiled. 'Thank you—but please don't call me "madam". It sounds so formal.' She glanced at Marc. Was she putting her foot in it already? Mrs Morelle laughed.

'Perhaps I might call you Mrs Marcus then? When I worked here many years ago the doctors' wives were called by their husbands' Christian names to avoid confusion.' She shook her head. 'But here I am chatting, and you'll be wanting your breakfast. I'll get on with it at once.'

Marc moved to the door. 'I have some work to do. If anyone wants me I'll be in the study.'

As the door closed behind him, Abigail looked hesitantly at the housekeeper. 'May I stay and help you? Or perhaps you don't welcome visitors in your kitchen.'

Mrs Morelle looked at her with raised eyebrows. 'But you're not a visitor. This is *your* kitchen—not mine.'

Abigail felt her cheeks colouring. 'Perhaps what I mean is that we should get to know one another—and while we're doing it I might as well make myself useful. I'm not used to standing around idle.'

The housekeeper laughed. 'I can see that you're going to make a very diplomatic doctor's wife!' She moved to the cupboard and began to busy herself with loading a tray. 'The first thing you can help with is to tell me what you like to eat for breakfast.'

'I usually make do with fruit juice and cereal,' Abigail told her. 'In my work I don't often get time for more than that anyway.'

'I see.' Mrs Morelle looked at her. 'And what would your work be?'

'I'm a nurse—a midwife.' So Marc hadn't told her? Maybe he hadn't told anyone. To him it was probably irrelevant! 'I think you said you used to work here many years ago, Mrs Morelle,' she said. 'Marc didn't tell me that.'

The housekeeper looked surprised. 'He didn't? I used to be his nanny when he was very small—from birth, in fact. Just before he went away to school I married and went to live on the mainland, but I was widowed five years ago and when I heard that Dr Stephen was looking for a housekeeper I applied.' She smiled reminiscently. 'It was lovely to come back to Guernsey again—like coming home. And to see that little boy I once knew, grown into a fine, handsome man—and a doctor too! Well, it almost made up for not having had any children of my own.' She smiled at Abigail. 'It's good to see him married and settled. I'm sure you're just the one for him, if you don't mind my saying so. You make such a good couple.'

Abigail sighed. This woman knew Marc so well. How would they manage to deceive her into believing that they were happy? Eager for a change of subject she said,

'You'll have to show me the house properly. So far I've only seen a few of the rooms.'

She bit her lip as she saw the housekeeper's knowing little smile. Obviously she was assuming that they had had better things to do with their wedding night than tour the house. Little did she know!

'Of course. I'll be delighted to show you round whenever you like,' she said. 'Though I expect Dr Marcus will be wanting to take you down to the surgery and show you off as soon as you've had breakfast.' She picked up the tray and looked enquiringly at Abigail. 'Now—will you take it on the terrace? It's a beautiful morning.'

They sat down to breakfast in silence. The long windows of the dining-room were open on to a wide, paved terrace with steps leading down to the lawn that Abigail had seen from her room. On a trellis against the wall, honeysuckle was in full bloom and the morning air was heavy with its fragrance. Marc looked at her as she poured the coffee.

'You seem to have made a hit with Morrie.'

She glanced at him. 'Thank you for taking the blame for the broken cup.'

He shook his head. 'It was my fault—I startled you. Anyway, it's not important.' He picked up the newspaper and began to read while she tried to swallow some of the food on her plate. Her throat felt tight and her stomach churned with apprehension. The best she could hope for was that Marc's cold manner would eventually freeze up the love she felt for him. It wasn't a happy prospect. He pushed away his empty plate and glanced at hers.

'Is that all you're going to eat?'

'I don't seem to have any appetite this morning.'

He rolled up his napkin and put it on the table. 'Right—shall we go then?' He stood up and looked down at her.

'Would you mind telling me where we're going?' she asked.

He sighed. 'To the surgery—I thought you'd realise that.' He looked at his watch in an impatient gesture. 'Are you ready? If you don't mind, I'd really like to make a start.'

For a moment she stared at him. He seemed to have no idea what he was asking of her. Meeting new in-laws was an ordeal at the best of times. Under her circumstances the ordeal was trebled. She rose to her feet with a sigh. She had agreed to his proposal—she had no choice but to see it through.

As they drove to the surgery she glanced at his profile. This morning he looked subtly different. There was a new hardness about his mouth and the golden eyes seemed several shades darker. With dismay she realised that this new remoteness only made her feeling for him stronger. She looked at the hands that held the wheel— strong, sensitive hands with long fingers and scrupulously manicured nails. Her heart turned over as she remembered the touch of those hands—a touch she might never know again. She thought about their conversation this morning. He had been so detached, so cold. Not once had he denied her accusations— protested that he loved her. It now seemed bleakly certain that what Aunt Honoria had told her was true.

He turned to her. 'Are you all right?'

She nodded, taking a deep breath. 'Don't worry. I won't let you down.'

He turned the car in through an open pair of white gates and parked in a paved yard. Switching off the engine he turned to look at her. 'Abby, I appreciate what you're doing, I want you to know that. You will try to—to smile, won't you?'

She bit hard on her lower lip to prevent herself from asking what she could possibly have to smile about; from demanding to know if he realised what torture this was for her. With every ounce of control she could muster she said, 'I'll try.'

The surgery was a modern, single storey building, and as they went in through double glass doors a reception desk faced them. A pretty, auburn-haired girl looked up and smiled delightedly.

'Dr Marcus! We were wondering whether you'd be in this morning.' She glanced at Abigail. 'Congratulations, Mrs DeLisle,' she said pleasantly.

'This is Sarah, our receptionist,' Marc told her. 'She sorts out all the terrible muddles they get into here and she also has a wonderfully soothing effect on the patients.' He grinned disarmingly at the girl. 'It's great to see you, Sarah. Is Dr Simon in yet?'

'He's in his surgery, and so is Dr Lesley.' Abigail noticed that the girl looked at Marc with the same wistful admiration as the nurses at Rinkley—cheeks pink and eyes shining. His charm seemed infallible.

Marc shot out his hand and covered hers. 'Don't buzz them. We'll make it a surprise.' Putting his hand under her elbow he guided her along a corridor to a door marked *Doctor Simon DeLisle*. Glancing at her briefly, he threw it open and walked in, one hand firmly on her arm, almost as though he expected her to cut and run.

The man who sat behind the desk was tall and well built. At once Abigail could see the family resemblance in the tanned skin and warm brown eyes, and she guessed that the thick silver hair had once been the same colour as Marc's. Dr Simon's handsome face broke into a smile as he rose to his feet and came round the desk to them, hands outstretched.

'Well, well, Marc, my dear boy! Welcome home!' He grasped both of Marc's hands and pressed them warmly, then he turned to Abigail. 'And to you too, my dear. I was so delighted to hear the news. Welcome to the DeLisle family.' Reaching out, he took her hand and held it, along with Marc's, in his own two. 'This calls for a celebration!' he laughed. 'Though I'm afraid that at this time of the morning and just before surgery we'll have to make do with coffee!' He went to his desk and pressed the intercom button. 'Sarah—can you rustle us up some coffee? Oh, and ask Dr Lesley to come in for a minute, will you?' He turned back to them. 'Now, tell me, how did the wedding go? Lesley and I were so sorry not to have been there. But we've a special do laid on for you this weekend. Lesley will tell you all about it. She's been busy arranging it all. A barbecue at the beach house—but I'd better not tell you any more and steal her thunder.

The door opened and Sarah came in with the tray of coffee. She glanced at Simon apologetically.

'I'm sorry to have to remind you, Doctor, but your first appointment is in fifteen minutes.'

He sighed. 'I know—I know.' He grinned at Abigail. 'Sometimes this girl is quite maddeningly efficient. I have a sneaking suspicion she likes to see people jumping about!'

As she was going out, Sarah almost collided with someone coming in. She stood back. 'Oh, Dr Lesley. I've just brought the coffee in. Will you pour? I'd better get back to the telephone.'

Abigail turned to see a tall, slim woman standing in

the doorway. Her raven dark hair was cut in a smooth shining cap which framed the heart-shaped face. Her deep violet eyes were looking straight at Marc, and it was impossible not to recognise the joy that shone in them. She answered Sarah briefly, then spoke Marc's name. He turned and noticed her, and Abigail saw the girl's delight mirrored in his own eyes as he held out his arms.

'Lesley!' She threw herself into his arms, winding her own around his neck and hugging him close.

'Oh, Marc—it's wonderful to have you home at last and to think we're going to be working together!' She kissed him soundly. Then, over his shoulder, she seemed to notice Abigail for the first time. She released her hold on Marc. 'And this is your wife—Abigail, isn't it? Welcome to King's Rock!'

She held out her hand and Abigail stepped forward hesitantly. Lesley seemed totally oblivious of the effect her greeting of Marc had created. Quite clearly they were accustomed to displaying their affection for each other in this way. Abigail swallowed the sharp surge of jealousy that rose in her mouth like a bitter taste, and forced herself to smile at the other girl.

'It's nice to meet you,' she said, taking the offered hand. 'I've heard so much about you.' She couldn't help glancing at Marc as she said the words, acutely aware of their irony. Hadn't she complained only last night that she hadn't been told enough?

Marc stepped forward, his eyes still on Lesley. 'I believe I told you that Abigail was a midwife? She'd like to continue working and she wondered if there might be a vacancy here for her.'

Lesley turned to Abigail with a dazzling smile. 'Is there a vacancy!' She looked at her father. 'Did you hear that, Dad? My dear, you couldn't have arrived at a more opportune moment! One of our midwives has just gone down with a bad attack of hepatitis. It looks as though she'll be out of action for at least six months. If you could fill in for her it would be marvellous!' She glanced at Marc doubtfully. 'Oh—but surely you don't want me whisking your bride away when you're still on your honeymoon? Weren't you planning a break before you start work?'

He shook his head. 'No time. By the look of the work snowing poor Uncle Simon under, I'd better get down to it as soon as I can. Actually, I was all set to stay on this morning if you want me.'

Dr Simon DeLisle and his daughter exchanged glances. 'Well, I won't pretend that the pressure isn't on,' Simon said at last. 'It would certainly be a relief to have some help. But are you quite sure?' He looked at Abigail. 'My dear child! It hardly seems fair. You should at least have had today to be together and settle down in your new home.'

Abigail blushed unhappily as they all three turned to look at her. 'Don't worry about me," she said, shaking her head. 'My father was a doctor too, so I've always known what to expect. Perhaps I can start work today too?' She looked hopefully at Lesley, who laughed, turning to Marc.

'Where did you find this paragon? You knew what you were doing when you picked her, didn't you?' She threw an arm around Abigail's shoulders. 'We'll have to get you kitted out with a uniform and a car, then you can come with me on my rounds if you like, and get to know the patients.'

Simon drained the last of his coffee and looked at his watch. 'And now I'm going to have to throw you all out.

My first patient will no doubt be sitting in the waiting room at this very minute.' He looked gratefully at Marc. 'You'll be taking over your father's surgery, of course. You'll be wanting to make a few changes, I know, but I've taken the liberty of having a name-plate made for the door. Perhaps I could divert Stephen's old patients to you. I'll have a word with Sarah.'

Lesley steered Abigail into the corridor. As she closed the surgery door behind her she smiled ruefully at her new midwife. 'That's the last you'll see of your husband for the rest of the day, I'm afraid. It's a good job you're so understanding. Now—are you really serious about wanting to begin right away?'

Abigail nodded. 'I don't know what else to do, so I might as well get my hand in.'

Out in the yard they climbed into Lesley's car, a bright yellow Citroën Dyane. 'Everyone calls this the biscuit tin,' she announced cheerfully. 'But I don't care. It has the advantage that it's nippy and easy on the petrol. Being bright yellow, people can see me coming and get out of the way too!' she laughed.

As they drove she explained to Abigail the way that she and her father worked. 'I take all the mums and babies, clinics—ante-natal, baby and so on. I'm hoping to specialise in obstetrics one of these days, so it's marvellous experience for me. If I didn't have a father who's a GP I don't suppose I'd get such opportunities, so I mean to make the most of them. We still have quite a number of home confinements here,' she told Abigail. 'We haven't tried to phase them out as they have on the mainland. What are your views on that?'

'Where I—Marc and I—have been working, in the Midlands, they encourage the short-stay confinement,' Abigail explained. 'I was a community midwife. We see the patient through the whole of the pregnancy and then when she goes into labour we go with her into hospital and deliver her there. She stays on for anything up to five days, depending on the case, being visited by us during that time, and then we follow her up at home. It seems to work very well. The perfect compromise, in fact, with fathers being encouraged to be present at the birth if they wish.'

Lesley nodded approvingly. 'It certainly sounds like a good idea. If I'm here long enough perhaps I shall be able to persuade the powers that be to adopt the idea.' She turned to smile at Abigail. 'How long have you know Marc?'

Abigail felt a slow flush creep up her neck. Talking about her work had made her forget her shyness for a while and almost obliterated the memory of last night's trauma. 'Not that long,' she said guardedly.

'Love at first sight, eh?'

'Something like that.' Abigail turned to look out of the window at the passing scenerey.

There was a pause and then Lesley said, 'I was engaged, but it didn't work out. We were working at the same hospital—in London.'

Abigail glanced at her. 'I'm sorry.'

Lesley shrugged. 'I've been spoilt, I suppose, having such marvellous men around me while I was growing up—Dad, Uncle Stephen, and of course, Marc.' She smiled ruefully at Abigail. 'But I don't have to tell you how wonderful *he* is, do I?'

'No.' Abigail chewed her lip, on the point of probing to see just how much Marc's cousin knew about her late uncle's will, but the moment passed as the other girl said,

'You'll be interested in the case we're going to see first this morning. She's thirty-eight and has a long history of miscarriages. She's coming into her seventh month now and she's just come out of hospital where she's been having a rest. She's rather an anxious patient—feels this might be her last chance to have a baby—so she tends to be a little tense; blood pressure rather on the high side and so on.'

'Toxaemia?' Abigail asked. Lesley shook her head.

'Not so far. That's why she's been in for a rest. I think we're winning, but you never know.' She turned off the road into a little lane and drew up outside a small house with a pretty garden.

'Just a few weeks ago I had a forty-three-year-old first-time mother,' Abigail remarked. 'Marc and I were quite anxious about her, but everything went perfectly.'

Lesley released her seat-belt and smiled. 'I'd be grateful if you'd tell Charlotte West that! Anyway, come and meet her.'

They made several calls after the Wests', finishing up with a visit to the maternity ward of the hospital at King's Rock where Lesley had four newly-delivered mothers. Abigail was introduced to the Sister and staff, who agreed that Lesley was lucky to have her as a replacement for the sick midwife, but Abigail couldn't help wondering if they would have been so free with their compliments had she not been the wife of their beloved Dr Marcus!

As they came down the steps of the hospital Lesley asked, 'Is Morrie expecting you back to lunch?'

Abigail frowned. 'Oh—how stupid of me. I didn't think to ask. I'm not used to having servants to consider!'

Lesley laughed. 'I've never thought of Morrie as a servant.'

'Oh, I only meant—' Abigail trailed off, her cheeks scarlet, and Lesley touched her arm.

'I just meant because she's so motherly. I suggest you go back to the house in case she's prepared something.'

'Yes. I don't want to get into her bad books this soon.' Abigail looked at the other girl. 'Will you join me? I don't suppose Marc will put in an appearance and there's bound to be enough for two.'

Lesley smiled. 'I'd love to.'

At DeLisle House Lesley seemed perfectly at home, running through to the kitchen to greet Mrs Morelle effusively. 'Hi, Morrie! I've been invited to lunch by the new Mrs DeLisle. What have you got for us? I hope there's a lot. I'm as hungry as a hunter!' She lifted the saucepan lids to peer inside and Mrs Morelle slapped her wrist, smiling at Abigail who stood in the doorway.

'These DeLisles never change—never grow up. I suppose there isn't any hope of Doctor coming in?'

'I told you, not a chance,' Lesley put in. 'So you can divide his between us two, and if he does come—well, serve him right for neglecting his lovely new bride!'

As they ate in the pleasant dining-room overlooking the garden, Lesley looked up. 'I haven't asked you yet how you liked the bridal suite.' Abigail lifted an enquiring eyebrow and she went on, 'Your room—and Marc's. He wanted it redecorated ready for you and he asked me to see to it. I hope it was to your taste.'

Abigail's heart sank at the thought of that room upstairs, the scene of last night's disaster. 'Oh, yes—it's lovely,' she said. 'Thank you for going to so much trouble.'

Lesley regarded her thoughtfully. 'You're very lucky, you know.'

Abigail looked up sharply. 'Lucky?'

'Yes. To have Marc. To be married to someone with whom you can share so much. It's what every woman wants, isn't it?' She looked up with a bright smile. 'Did Dad tell you I've organised a barbecue at the beach house for this Saturday evening? You'll be able to meet all Marc's friends and colleagues in one fell swoop and get it over with. I think it will be a very pleasant evening and I'm sure the weather will hold. Don't forget to bring your bikini. The sea is already quite warm—I tried it myself the other evening.' She rose from the table, dabbing the corners of her mouth with a napkin. 'That reminds me, I'll have a word with Morrie while I'm here about the food. Excuse me, will you?'

When she had gone, Abigail sat staring out of the window at the idyllic green of the lawn and the bright flowers in the borders. She felt like a stranger in this house that was supposed to be her home. 'The new Mrs DeLisle.' The phrase echoed mockingly in her ears. Lesley had arranged everything—the barbecue, the decor . . . The place seemed more hers than Abigail's. Perhaps she would like it to be—expected it. Abigail saw again the wistful expression in her eyes when she had said, 'To be married to someone with whom one can share so much—it's what every woman wants.' She remembered the look in her eyes when she had welcomed Marc home, and his response. Lesley wasn't her rival, she told herself. There was really no contest. She had already won the battle for Marc—if only she knew it!

CHAPTER SIX

ABIGAIL sat before the white-frilled dressing-table. It was Saturday evening and she was getting ready for the barbecue. She had been at DeLisle House for a week—seven days of torture, broken only by the blessing of work—and now, this evening, she had to face the ordeal of meeting all the DeLisle family's friends.

On that first evening Marc had not arrived home until eight o'clock. He had looked tired and it had occurred to her that he had probably worked late at the surgery to avoid her. Mrs Morelle served dinner to them in the dining-room, then went home to her own cottage, leaving them tactfully alone. The meal over, Marc had thanked her coolly for her efforts that morning, then withdrawn to his study where he had stayed until long after she was in bed. She heard him moving about in the dressing-room next door and assumed that he had decided to sleep in there on the divan.

On the subsequent days they had breakfasted together and gone to their respective work. In the evenings they kept up the pretence for Mrs Morelle's benefit, but otherwise kept out of each other's way. After a week of this Abigail felt she could stand it no longer. The situation was intolerable. Marc might find it easier—after all he had been playing the part from the first, hadn't he?—but for Abigail the past seven days had felt more like years. The months ahead stretched before her like a prison sentence. She made up her mind. She must speak to Marc about it—now!

She could hear him moving about in the dressing-room adjoining. Taking her courage in both hands, she stood up and drew on her bathrobe, then crossed the room and tapped on the door.

'Marc, may I speak to you?'

There was a slight pause, then he opened the door. He too wore a bathrobe, and his hair was damp from a recent shower, clinging to his neck in tight curls. She caught a whiff of his sharp, spicy aftershave.

He looked at her enquiringly. 'Yes?'

She turned away into the room so that he would not see her despairing look. 'Marc, I'm not sure that I can keep this up—this awful play-acting.'

He didn't move from the doorway. 'Really? I thought you were doing rather well.'

She turned to look at him and saw that he was smiling lazily, one eyebrow raised.

'Then I must be a better actress than I thought!' she retorted. 'I can't live like this for a whole year. I can't live a lie.'

He walked into the room and crossed to the window to stand gazing out. After a moment he turned to look at her. 'All right. What do you propose?'

She shrugged unhappily. 'I don't know—I thought you might. At least we could talk about it.'

He sat down in the little velvet chair by the bed, stretching his long legs out before him. 'Tell me, Abby. That night—the night of the wedding—what did you intend to do? You knew then, so you must have had some plan of action.'

She could feel the tears knotting her throat and she turned to him again. 'I believe you enjoy it,' she told him, 'this game of cat and mouse. You knew that I was in love with you. You took advantage of that for your own convenience, and when I found out and faced you with it you didn't like it.'

He stood up quickly, his eyes flashing dangerously. 'How dare you say that? How dare you accuse me?'

She spun round to face him, anger and humiliation sinking their talons into her heart. 'You must have thought you'd done well, finding a stupid little fool like me who'd follow you to the ends of the earth and fall in with anything you asked, especially one who knew the world of medicine, who understood and would make no demands, leaving you free to do whatever you wanted. If I hadn't found out—what then? Would you still have thrown me out after a year—after you'd paid the price for your glittering prize?'

His hands shot out to grasp her shoulders and she shrank from the fury that emanated from him. Inside her, despair shrivelled the anger that had made her lash out. It had all gone wrong. She hadn't meant to say all that—to let her bitterness spill over. She had meant it to be a civilised discussion; for them to formulate some plan that would make the coming months more tolerable. The trouble was that she couldn't look at him without the pain of wanting him—without the grinding hurt of his betrayal crushing her.

'You've made up your mind. You don't want to hear any other version but your own, do you?' His eyes had darkened to the colour of granite as he looked down at her. 'Compromise is an unknown word to you, with your narrow little mind!'

She stared up at him challengingly. 'All right—so tell me your side. Tell me there was no marriage clause in your father's will!'

He stiffened and she saw the colour leave his face. His nostrils flared as he looked down at her. 'No, I'm not going to tell you that. I'm not a liar. You were right about the clause.'

'So it *was* true. He had finally admitted it. Abigail felt her lower lip drop with surprise as she stared up into his eyes, then she wrenched herself from his grip and turned away.

'I'm not coming tonight—I can't. You can tell them I'm ill—tell them anything you like.'

'I'll do nothing of the kind. You *are* coming.' He crossed the room to where her dress hung and snatched it from its hanger, thrusting it at her. 'Put that on and stop behaving like a spoilt child!'

She could feel a sob rising in her chest, but she swallowed it back. She would *not* show him how much he was hurting her. 'How can you speak of *compromise*?' she flung at him. 'All the compromise is to be on my side, isn't it? You tell me what to do and I do it! You pull the strings and I play the part of your loving wife—until it's time to be thrown into the corner when the show's over! Well I won't do it!'

'And what *will* you do, Abby?' he asked her tauntingly. 'Go back to Rinkley, perhaps, and tell everyone the whole thing was a mistake—that you were conned? All I'm asking is that you stay here in comparative comfort for twelve months, after which you can make a new start with my help. Which do you honestly believe is the most sensible?'

'I *hate* you!' She bit her lip to quell the desire to slap the cool expression from his face.

His eyebrows rose. 'Not five minutes ago you were telling me that you were in love with me!'

Her hand rose but he caught it, gripping her wrist painfully. He stepped closer to her. 'Abby—for God's sake try to be reasonable,' he said. 'If we're going to get through the coming months with our sanity intact, we've got to behave like adults.' He looked at her, seeing the tears standing in her eyes, feeling her capitulation as the tension seeped out of her body. The hard lines of his face softened and he bent to pick up her dress from the floor where it had fallen. 'You'd better get into this. It's almost time we were going.' At the door he turned to look at her. 'Don't worry. You'd be surprised how time can fly. Before you know it you'll be free again.'

She stared at the door for a long moment, then turned to the mirror, sinking on to the dressing-table stool, her knees suddenly weak. She was trapped. There was nothing she could do. 'You'll soon be free,' he had said. Why couldn't he see that she'd never be free again? She drew a deep breath. 'I won't let him see that he has the power to crush me,' she told her reflection. 'If I have to play a part I'll play it well. I won't let him see how unhappy I am!'

She made up her face carefully, disguising the dark shadows under her eyes that spoke of sleepless nights. She brushed on plenty of blusher and chose the brightest lipstick she had, then she slipped into the crisp white broderie anglaise dress and brushed her hair until it shone.

He was waiting for her at the bottom of the stairs, looking heart-stoppingly handsome in linen slacks and a blue cotton shirt. She held her head high as she walked past him.

'I hope I haven't kept you waiting too long?' she said with a hint of irony.

He smiled with icy politeness. 'Not at all.'

The beach house was really an old stone fisherman's cottage built over a century ago at the foot of the cliff. A winding sandy path led from it to the beach where Lesley had set up the barbecue. Long trestle tables were loaded with bowls of salad of every kind, and baskets piled high with crusty bread. Simon DeLisle, looking bronzed and fit in his shorts and T-shirt was busy cooking steaks, while Lesley counted out plates and paper napkins. She also wore shorts and a bikini top, revealing her tanned body and shapely legs. Her dark hair clung damply to her head. When she saw Marc and Abigail she called out cheerfully, 'Hi, you two! I've just been for a swim. Thought I'd better try out the water. It's great!'

'Can I help with all this?' Abigail asked, looking round for something to do to ease her nervousness. Lesley looked shocked.

'I should just think not! You, my dear girl, are the guest of honour tonight. Don't worry, your turn will come soon enough. I expect you realise that everyone will be expecting you to give a dinner party as soon as you've had time to settle in?'

Abigail blushed. 'No, I hadn't as a matter of fact.'

Lesley looked at her askance. 'But of course! They'll all be dying to see what the new mistress of DeLisle House has done to put her stamp on things!' She laughed at Abigail's expression. 'Don't look so terrified, love. I'll be here to help you.'

Abigail felt a stab of irritation. Why should Lesley naturally assume that she couldn't cope? If she had to give a dinner party for Marc's friends and colleagues, then she would do it—and do it well. That was the least of her problems!

Marc was looking out across the smooth water of the bay. 'I see you've got the raft out,' he remarked. Lesley nodded.

'Yes. Dad towed it out and anchored it this after-noon.'

'We must swim out to it later.' Marc smiled at Abigail. 'Funny, I've never asked you if you like swimming. Here, it's so much a part of summer living that we take it for granted.'

Lesley smiled at her. 'You can change in the beach house—but not just yet.' She turned to look up at the cliff path. 'I believe I can hear the first of the guests arriving.'

For the hour that followed they arrived thick and fast—people of all ages, married and single. There were children and even the odd dog or two. Without exception they were all delighted to welcome Abigail, and for a while she almost forgot her unhappiness as they greeted her warmly. Many of them went to the beach house to change and made for the water, while others were more interested in Lesley's delicious food.

Soon it became a relaxed gathering, guests sitting or lying on the golden sand or standing in groups around the smoking barbecue chatting happily to Simon as he cooked. Marc had played the part of the attentive husband to perfection, holding Abigail's hand tenderly and guiding her among the guests with a look of pride in his eyes. No one would have guessed at the scene that had preceded the party. She found it all a strain, and when at last he fell into a serious discussion with an elderly colleague from King's Rock Hospital she crept away. Helping herself to a glass of lemonade, she sat on a smooth rock at the base of the cliff, glad of a breather.

'Hello—what's all this? The blushing bride left to blush unseen?'

Abigail looked up to find a pair of grey eyes smiling down at her. They belonged to Alan Blake, a young man Marc had introduced earlier as the son of the family's solicitor. He eased himself on to the rock beside her and looked at her glass of lemonade with distaste. 'What's that muck you're drinking? And why haven't you got anything to eat?' He held out his own loaded plate to her. 'Here, you have this and I'll go and get some more.'

She shook her head. 'No, really. I'm not hungry, thanks.'

He assumed a look of disapproval. 'Not hungry? We can't have that!' His eyes swept over the slim figure. 'It can't be that you're slimming. If you are, I can assure you that there's no need.'

'No, I'm not slimming.' She was beginning to feel irritated and wished he would go away, but he settled himself more comfortably and began to tuck into his steak and salad, obviously determined to keep her company. He was quite good-looking in a rakish kind of way, with dark hair that flopped over his brow and a neatly-trimmed moustache. He glanced up at her, his eyes twinkling.

'I suppose you should be circulating, but I'm glad you're not. It means that I can monopolise you!'

Abigail looked round. 'Surely there's someone looking for you? Didn't you bring a friend?'

'No.' He laid a hand on her arm. 'I'll let you into a secret. My girlfriend and I had a row last night.'

'Oh dear. I'm so sorry.'

'Don't be. It means I'm footloose and fancy free again—my favourite position!' He grinned at her as he set aside his empty plate. 'Are you going in for a swim?'

She shrugged. 'I might later.'

'Great.' He looked at her thoughtfully. 'Marc's a lucky devil. Knows how to pick 'em—and finding a girl in the same line as himself too! But then he's a good-looking so-and-so, isn't he?' He looked across to where Marc was talking to Lesley, helping her to stack plates.

'There was a time when I thought that he and Lesley—'
he muttered, half to himself. 'But then that wouldn't
have done for Stephen—oh no, not at all! So maybe it's
just as well that you came along to fill the bill so neatly,
eh?'

Abigail didn't care for the way the conversation was
going. She stood up and brushed down her skirt. 'I think
I'll go up to the house and change for that swim,' she
said.

He looked up at her lazily. 'Oh, I'd join you if I hadn't
just eaten. What a pity. Maybe I'll see you again later?'

'Yes—maybe.' She was already half-way up the path.
Did everyone know about Marc and his cousin? Were
they all comparing her with the glamorous and gifted
Lesley?

Abigail changed in the small bathroom at the beach
house, then stood looking at herself critically in the long
mirror over the bath. She didn't have Lesley's golden
tan; her legs weren't as long either. She tugged at the
brief bikini, wishing she'd brought a one-piece swimsuit
instead, to hide all that pale skin. Hesitantly she began
to push open the door, then stopped as she heard voices
in the corridor outside. She recognised Lesley's voice
saying, 'I really think she had a right to know, Marc.'

'Why—what difference could it make?' he asked.
'The fewer people who know, the better. We've always
agreed on that. If it leaked out it would only be a matter
of time before Simon got to hear, and that's the last thing
you want, isn't it?'

'I know, but all the same—' There was a pause, then
she said, 'You haven't done anything to upset her, have
you? She doesn't seem very happy.'

Abigail bit her lip; they *were* talking about her.

'Of course I haven't!' Marc sounded defensive.

'I only ask because there's something about her—a sort of preoccupation,' Lesley went on. 'She's a sensitive, perceptive girl—a damned good midwife, if I'm any judge. I wondered if you'd given her any reason to suspect—about us, I mean?'

'What do you take me for?'

'You're a bit of a chauvinist, Marc, in spite of all that charm of yours. Abby isn't a fool. How do you think you're going to keep something like that from a wife? It's a very close relationship, after all.'

'You've managed to keep it from Simon,' he countered. 'And you and he have always been close enough—' A door slammed and the voices were abruptly cut off. Abigail stepped out into the hallway. She could hear a faint murmur coming from behind the closed kitchen door and the muffled sounds of washing-up. Obviously Marc was helping Lesley to wash plates and glasses. Quickly and silently she ran out through the open door and down on to the beach again, her heart thudding in her chest. If only she could get away from all these people—run as far as she could from this place. The best she could do was to swim.

Skirting the crowd, she ran into the calm water till it reached her waist, then struck out for the raft that was rising and falling in the slight swell about a hundred yards from the shore. The water felt cool and silky and she was grateful for its soothing caress on her skin. At last she reached the raft and pulled herself up on to it. She was out of breath and lay still for a while until her breathing returned to normal. The words of the conversation she had overheard rang in her head, and she rolled on to her back to stare up at the sky.

What was it that Lesley felt she should know—and that Marc seemed equally determined to keep from her?

The answer was obvious. Clearly Marc intended to continue his relationship with Lesley, but it would not be in anyone's interest to allow it to be common knowledge yet. First his marriage must be firmly established and then cancelled. He must think Lesley well worth waiting for; well worth the sacrifice of another human heart. For the hundredth time Abigail wondered how she would bear the months to come. At that moment the humiliation of returning home seemed almost inviting by comparison.

'You seem determined to be alone! Can all those soap ads be true after all?'

She started as a dark head appeared over the edge of the raft. Sitting up, she saw Alan Blake smiling at her as he shook the water from his hair. He heaved his long body out of the sea to sit beside her. 'You're looking very pensive. Is anything wrong?'

Abigail shrank under his frankly admiring gaze, wishing she had a towel to wrap around herself. 'Does there have to be something wrong with a person who likes a little solitude?' she asked. His eyebrows rose.

'Not unless she happens to be a bride,' he said meaningly. 'Where is the lucky man, by the way?'

She shrugged. 'We don't have to live like Siamese twins just because we happen to be married!'

He grinned. 'It's a delicious thought though, isn't it?' He regarded her thoughtfully. 'Look, Abigail—I may call you that, I hope? I hope I'm not offending you when I tell you that I know a little more about your situation than most people and, frankly, I got rather a surprise when I met you this evening.'

'Oh? What did you expect—two heads?' She felt suddenly vulnerable and folded her arms across her chest in an involuntary gesture of protection. Glancing at him coolly she said, 'I don't think I care to discuss it with you if you don't mind.'

He reached out to touch her shoulder. 'Fair enough. But remember that my father is Marc's solicitor and I hope to join the firm as soon as I've passed my finals. Any time you do want to talk I hope you'll look on me as a friend as well as a solicitor. Someone in whom you can confide and trust.'

Abigail stood up. 'Thanks, but I honestly can't envisage needing anyone like that at the moment.' She dived into the smooth water and began to swim strongly towards the shore. It was hateful to think of people knowing how and why she came to be here—even Alan, the ethics of whose profession forbade him to tell anyone else.

As she reached the shallows she stood up and waded ashore. Someone called, 'Here she is!' and Simon stepped forward and held out his hand to her.

'Ah, there you are my dear. We've been looking for you. Marc has just had a telephone call. He has to go and see a patient but he didn't want to leave until he'd seen you.' He looked round. 'Here he is now.'

Marc carried a beach wrap which he threw around her shoulders. 'I've been called out, I'm afraid,' he told her. 'It sounds quite serious and I may be some time.'

She looked up at him, her lip trembling a little with cold. 'I see—thank you for finding me and letting me know.'

His hands were strong and she could feel their warmth through the material of the beach robe. His grip tightened as he felt her tremble. 'You're cold.' He looked down at her solicitously. 'Get dressed now. I dare say Simon will see you home safely.'

'Don't worry, Marc. I'll see she gets home.' The voice

was Alan's. He had swum back from the raft after her and stood behind Abigail on the sand. Marc nodded to him.

'Thanks,' he said curtly. 'Well, I'll see you in the morning, Abby. Don't wait up for me.'

She tried to smile, acutely aware that a dozen pairs of eyes were watching them. Clearly Marc was aware of this too, for he suddenly drew her to him and kissed her full on the mouth. She caught her breath as the warmth of him enveloped her—at the strength and sweetness of his lips on hers. She resisted the urge to cling to him, but as their lips parted she brushed her cheek briefly against his. Then he was gone, calling his goodbyes to the guests as he ran up the beach while Abigail stood looking wistfully after him.

'You'd better do as he said like a good little wife, hadn't you?' She felt Alan's arm heavy on her shoulders and looked up.

'Yes, I suppose so. I am feeling a little chilly.'

He looked around. 'People seem to be dwindling away now anyway. I'll get dressed and wait for you.'

She dressed hurriedly and said good night to Lesley and Simon, then circulated among the remaining guests, saying her goodbyes and thanking them for coming. Now that the sun had finally gone it was chilly on the beach. The sand felt clammy under her bare feet and a stiff little breeze coming off the water made her shiver. Alan was waiting by his car, a racey red two-seater. He helped her in and they began the steep climb up the sandy cliff road. As he pulled on to the main road at the top he glanced at her.

'Sure you want to go straight home?'

She looked at him in surprise. 'Quite sure, thanks.'

He shrugged. 'Just thought you might fancy a brandy if you're feeling cold.'

'If I do there's plenty at home,' she told him.

'Is that an invitation by any chance?' He smiled at her cheekily, eyes twinkling, and she laughed in spite of herself.

'No, it isn't—though I'm sure Marc would want me to offer you a drink for seeing me safely home.'

His smile was wry as he said, 'I wouldn't take bets on it! He was very definitely staking his claim with that kiss, wasn't he? Don't think I didn't get the message!'

Abigail made no reply. Why had Marc kissed her? It was the first time since their arrival here a week ago. Almost certainly it had been for the benefit of those watching, because they had been expecting it and it would have looked odd not to have kissed her goodbye. But could he have known what it had done to her—the tumult of feeling it had awakened in her?

Alan drew up outside the front door of DeLisle House and switched off the engine, turning to look at her.

'Well, this is it, Mrs DeLisle. Cinderella's return from the ball—minus Prince Charming.' He leaned towards her, his arm along the back of the seat. 'Tell you what—you're tired. I'll take a rain check on that drink.'

She was grateful and relieved, but as she started to get out of the car he laid a hand on her arm. 'I meant what I said earlier, Abigail,' he said quietly. 'If ever you need a friend, remember I'm here.'

She turned to look at him. 'Thank you. I'll remember.'

His fingers began, very faintly, to caress her bare arm. 'I told you that I was surprised when I met you. I thought you'd be a little mouse of a girl—someone plain and insignificant who'd jump at Marc's offer. How wrong can you get? I have to admit, I'm curious.'

'Then you'll just have to go on being curious. I have no—' Before she could finish the sentence he had bent and kissed her swiftly.

'That's just to seal our friendship, Abby,' he said softly, his face still close to hers and his hand still on her arm. 'I hope we'll be seeing a lot of each other in the future.'

Her heart thudding uncomfortably, she extricated herself from his grasp and got out of the car. 'Thank you for the lift. Good night, Alan,' she said coolly.

In the dim hall of the empty house she stood with her back to the closed door, listening with relief to the sound of his car going away down the drive. How many more unscrupulous, so-called friends did Marc have, she wondered?

CHAPTER SEVEN

ABIGAIL DREW up outside the attractive small house she had visited with Lesley on her first day in King's Rock. Switching off the engine of the car she hesitated for a moment, then slipped it into gear. The brakes seemed a little unreliable and as the road sloped she didn't want to take any chances. When Marc had seen the car Lesley had managed to get for her as a temporary measure he had been appalled.

'That thing needs a thorough overhall. There's a perfectly good BMW standing idle in the garage,' he told her. 'Why don't you use that?'

But she had been adamant. As a local midwife she would use the car provided. Somehow she would find the time to get it serviced. What would the other midwives think if she drove around like a queen in a luxury car? It would look as though she were enjoying special privileges just because she happened to be married to Marcus DeLisle!

Reaching into the back for her case, she got out of the car and opened the front gate. She could see Charlotte West relaxing on a lounger on the front lawn under the shade of a lilac tree. When she saw Abigail coming she struggled to heave her bulk from the chair.

'Stay where you are,' Abigail called, smiling as she came up to her patient. 'Just tell me where I can find a chair too and we'll have a chat out here before we go inside for your check-up.'

She fetched a chair from the porch at the back of the

house and set it up next to Charlotte's, sinking into it with relief.

'Ah, that's bliss. It's really warm this morning, isn't it?' She looked at her patient, taking in the healthy tanned skin and generally glowing appearance. Pregnancy suited her. 'Well, only a matter of weeks to go now,' she smiled. 'How are you feeling, Charlotte?'

'Fine thanks—though I have to admit that I do get rather tired now.' Charlotte West pulled herself more upright on the lounger and looked at Abigail. 'When I saw Dr Lesley at the ante-natal clinic last week she was talking about taking me into hospital when the time comes, to have an epidural.'

Abigail nodded. 'That's partly why I'm here this morning. To tell you all about it,' she said. 'Of course, you don't have to have it, but Dr Lesley thinks that as you have a very narrow cervical canal it would make the birth much easier for you.'

Charlotte sighed. 'Paul and I have been discussing it, but he says it must be my choice in the end. The trouble is that I'm not sure what it involves.'

'It's really just a local anaesthetic,' Abigail told her. 'Into the epidural space which runs along the length of the spine and carries the nerves. The anaesthetic is fed into this space so that you can feel nothing below your waist, although of course you stay awake throughout the birth.'

Charlotte smiled. 'It sounds wonderful, but is it safe— for the baby, I mean?'

'In many ways safer than a general anaesthetic—for you both,' Abigail assured her. 'Some women complain that they miss the actual sensation of their baby's birth, but then you can't have everything. If you were unconscious you wouldn't experience it at all.'

Charlotte nodded. 'And you really think it's advisable?'

'As your husband says, it's your choice,' Abigail told her. 'But it could be necessary to do it anyway. The advantage of deciding now is that we could take you in on the day the baby is due and do a good deal of it in advance, before you actually go into labour—later it might not be as easy and relaxed for you.'

Charlotte looked puzzled. 'What exactly could you do in advance?'

'The small tube could be inserted—in your back at waist level,' Abigail explained. 'Ready for the anaesthetic to be inserted. It sounds awful, but I promise you it's quite a simple procedure and no more uncomfortable than an ordinary injection. But of course it's much easier to do it before the patient goes into labour.'

'I can imagine.' Charlotte smiled. 'Well, I don't think I need worry about it any more. I think I'll say yes now.'

'Good. I'll see that you're booked in and I'll tell Dr Lesley. I know she'll be glad that you've made the decision.' Abigail held out a hand to help Charlotte up from her chair. 'Shall we go inside now for your routine check?'

In the Wests' cool, pretty bedroom Abigail made the routine examination, happy to be able to note that Charlotte's blood pressure was remaining steady and that the position of her unborn child was normal. She smiled as she put away her stethoscope and sphygmomanometer. 'What are you hoping for, a boy or a girl?' she asked.

'Just so long as it's normal and healthy I don't care.' Charlotte slid her legs over the edge of the bed and sat up. 'You know, I feel really honoured—having Dr Marcus's wife looking after me.'

Abigail snapped her case shut and looked up sharply. 'I really don't see why being married to a doctor should make me a better midwife. I hope I was doing as good a job before I met him!' The words were sharper than she had intended and she was ashamed to see that she had embarrassed Charlotte. Immediately Aunt Honoria's words came to mind—'Those DeLisles—so arrogant, so proud!' It looked very much as though some of it was rubbing off on to her!

'I'm sorry, Charlotte,' she said, removing her disposable apron. 'That must have sounded rude. I didn't mean it to. It's just that I don't want to be thought of as someone special just because of the name.'

'I don't blame you,' Charlotte said. 'A lot of the mothers-to-be admire you for keeping up your career, though I think most of them were surprised. I think they saw Dr Marcus's wife as a sort of lady of leisure, socialising and occupying her time in beautifying DeLisle House. They say it was once the hub of social life around here, but since poor Dr Stephen lived there alone it's become rather neglected.'

Abigail held out her arm to help the patient on to her feet. 'Well, I hope all that can be remedied, but I'm afraid that I'd find a life of undiluted parties rather boring. I enjoy my job too much to be a social butterfly.'

Charlotte smiled. 'And I'm certainly grateful that you do. Have you got time for a coffee?'

Abigail looked at her watch and shook her head regretfully. 'I'd love to, but I'm running late this morning. Thanks a lot, but I'd better get on.'

Back in the car Abigail thought about what Charlotte had said. Lesley had remarked that people would be expecting her to 'put her stamp' on the place. So far she had been too preoccupied to give it much thought.

Anyway, under the circumstances she didn't feel that DeLisle House was really her home. A few months from now and she would be gone, so what was the use of imposing her own tastes?

As she drove her thoughts stayed with Lesley. She always seemed so at home at DeLisle House. Was she planning her own changes? Abigail wondered. Looking forward to the day when the house, as well as Marc, would be hers? Abigail pictured Lesley's attractive face and wished, not for the first time, that she could find it in her to dislike her. Since they had begun to work together she had grown more and more to like and admire the young woman doctor, appreciating her skill and tact with her patients, her caring manner and her infinite patience. It was no wonder she was so popular. She certainly deserved success in her career and to attain her ambition to specialise in obstetrics. Abigail could scarcely believe that she would give it all up to become the mistress of DeLisle House, but then one could never tell. The past few weeks had taught her to take nothing for granted.

The day grew hotter and more oppressive. That afternoon at the clinic the mothers-to-be were tired and irritable, fractious toddlers clinging to their skirts or squabbling over the box of toys in the play area. Even with all the windows open there seemed hardly any air to breathe, and by the end of the afternoon patients and staff were exhausted. As they walked out to the car park together, Abigail told Lesley of her talk with Charlotte West that morning and of her decision to have the epidural. Lesley looked pleased.

'That's a relief. I haven't mentioned it before, but we may have to deliver by Caesarean section. If she's already anaesthetised it will help a lot. Of course, a

Caesar would only be a last resort, so I don't intend to worry Charlotte by mentioning it at this stage.'

They reached Abigail's car and Lesley frowned. 'Haven't you taken this to be serviced yet?'

Abigail shook her head. 'I just haven't found the time. You know how busy we've been. It will have to wait until my next break.'

Lesley looked at her reprovingly. 'You know perfectly well you have the use of another car. Marc will never forgive me if anything happens to you. Promise me you'll get it seen to as soon as you can.'

Abigail flushed as she climbed into the Mini. Obviously they had been discussing her again. 'I hate being thought of as privileged,' she said. 'The patients already think I'm merely amusing myself to while away the time. I *am* a person in my own right as well as Marc's wife!'

Lesley smiled wryly. 'All right. You don't have to convince me. But isn't this carrying independence a little too far? You have to think of the safety aspect, you know. You're not going to be much use to the patients in a hospital bed, are you?'

Abigail switched on the ignition and revved the noisy little engine, ignoring Lesley's grimace. 'I've told you— I'll take it to be done when my break comes round,' she said stubbornly. 'It's no problem.'

She drove from the clinic to the centre of town, through the cobbled streets with their pretty Regency houses and out into the more modern suburbs. Even with the car windows open the heat was oppressive, and when she eventually emerged on to the coast road it was hardly any cooler. A mist hung over the bay, and as Abigail climbed the cliff road the sea below her looked like a sheet of silver, gleaming dully through the haze. The first drops of rain were like drum beats on the roof of the car, then a jagged flash of lightning crazed across the sky, followed in a few seconds by the rumble of thunder.

Abigail pressed her foot down hard on the accelerator. Storms made her uneasy. The sooner she could get back to DeLisle House, the better. The rain grew heavier. It rattled fiercely down on the roof of the little car, almost obscuring her vision as it streamed down the windscreen, defying the wipers. Another blinding flash made her blink, and the deafening crash of thunder that followed brought an involuntary cry from her lips, for it sounded immediately overhead.

She pressed her foot down on the brake, deciding to pull into the side of the road and wait until the storm had passed before continuing. To her horror, the footbrake did not respond to her pressure. The car skidded crazily across the wet road and Abigail's heart froze with fear as she tried in vain to bring it under control again. Ahead there was a sharp bend—she was travelling much too fast to negotiate it. Below, the sea had turned from silver to lead. She couldn't see the jagged rocks, but she knew they were there. Desperately she struggled with the wheel, but to no avail. As she approached the bend she tried to force the gear lever into a lower gear, but she couldn't manage this either. Heart in mouth, she watched the edge of the road come perilously close and made a frantic grab for the hand-brake. There was a scream of tyres and suddenly she was at a standstill.

The car creaked and rocked. The two off-side wheels hung over the edge of the cliff; only her own weight in the driving seat was preventing it from tipping sideways and sliding down the steep slope. Abigail sat petrified, frozen to the seat with fear. Once she attempted to shift her weight in an effort to reach the door handle, but the slight movement set the car rocking alarmingly. She heard loose stones break free from under the wheels and bounce down the cliffside. Above her the rain had eased and the thunder rumbled angrily in the distance. Then she heard another sound—a car was coming in the opposite direction.

She bit her lip hard, hoping that it wouldn't take the bend too wide. The driver wouldn't see her until the car was right on top of her. She pressed her hand hard on the horn, keeping it there in the hope that the driver would take it as a warning and slow down, and shut her eyes as a flash of red went past her. She heard the car pull up a few yards along the road, then the slam of a door and running feet. A man's voice called, 'Hang on! Don't try to move.'

The face that appeared at the car window was Alan Blake's. Abigail had never been so thankful to see a familiar face in her life before. With great care he opened the door, speaking calmly.

'Are you hurt?' She shook her head. 'Good. Slide your legs out—carefully, one at a time.' He held out his arm and she hooked her own gratefully round it, easing first one leg, then the other over the door sill. Alan looked at her and then, with one heave, he pulled her free. Behind her she heard a groan, then a crash as the car plunged over the edge of the cliff. She hid her face against Alan's shoulder as she listened to the splintering of wood as it cut a swathe through the growth of vegetation in its path, followed by the shattering of metal as it hit the rocks below. Alan patted her back.

'Are you all right?'

She looked up at him. 'I—think so. I can't thank you enough. If you hadn't come along at that moment—' A violent shudder shook her body and he slipped an arm around her.

'Come along. I'll take you home. You need a drink. We can ring the police from DeLisle House and report the accident.'

In his car she sat numbly, her teeth chattering as the reaction set in. Only one thought filled her mind. This evening she had almost died. If it were not for the man sitting beside her she would be lying at the bottom of the cliff at this moment, broken and lifeless—or perhaps terribly injured. She thought of Marc, of dying without seeing him again, and her eyes filled with tears. Alan's voice cut through her thoughts.

'What was Marc thinking about, letting you drive a heap like that?'

'Marc doesn't *let* me do things. I make my own decisions!' she said thickly. 'As a matter of fact he wanted me to use his father's BMW, but I didn't want to be different to anyone else.'

He looked at her wryly, one eyebrow raised. 'Well you very nearly were, weren't you? *Very* different!'

'All right. Don't rub it in.' She bit her lip as she looked at him. 'Sorry. I didn't mean to snap at you. You saved my life—I—' Tears began to slide helplessly down her cheeks.

'All right. Look, the first thing is to get you home to that husband of yours as soon as possible. Here, you'd better have this.' He handed her a large white handkerchief. As she took it from him a sudden thought struck her and she turned a dismayed face to him.

'Oh, Alan! My bag—with all my things—it was in the back of the car!'

'For God's sake, what does that matter as long as you're safe?'

He drove up to the front door of DeLisle House and came round to help her out. In the hall he shouted for

Mrs Morelle who came running in response to the urgency in his voice.

'What is it—is something wrong?' She took in Abigail's white, tearstained face. 'Oh, Mrs Marcus—whatever's happened?'

'She had a bit of a spill on the cliff road,' Alan explained. 'I'm afraid the car's a write-off. Is Marc about?'

'I'm afraid not. He telephoned to say he wouldn't be in to dinner—some meeting or other.'

Alan swore under his breath. 'Doctors! They're like policemen—never around when you need them!'

Mrs Morelle took Abigail by the arm. 'Come upstairs and lie down. I'll make you a nice cup of tea.'

'I'll ring the police,' Alan said. 'Will you feel up to giving them a statement later, Abby?'

She turned from the foot of the stairs. 'Yes, of course. I'm quite all right really. And please, both of you, I'd rather you didn't make too much of it to Marc.'

Alan stared at her. 'He's got to know you've had an accident! You're not hoping to keep it from him, surely?'

'No, but I'd rather tell him the details myself. I don't want a lot of fuss made about it.'

Lying on the bed in the darkened bedroom she felt suddenly exhausted. Mrs Morelle brought her a hot cup of tea and two aspirins. Later she brought her something to eat on a tray and told her that the police would be round for a statement in the morning. Abigail picked at the food but couldn't eat anything. Pushing the tray aside she got up and went into the bathroom. Bathed and undressed, she crept back into bed again and closed her eyes.

Coming here was the worst thing she could have done,

she told herself. Ever since the moment Marc and she had married everything had gone wrong. She rolled over despairingly, burying her face in the pillow. Perhaps it might have been better if Alan had *not* come along this afternoon. That would have been the end of all her problems—and Marc's too. Hot tears scalded her face and soaked into the pillow until she fell into an exhausted sleep.

As the hours passed she tossed and whimpered as disjointed splinters of dream sliced into her restlessness. She was staring down at an angry sea—lashing waves and flying spray—at evil-looking rocks. She was moving much too fast in a car that had no steering wheel and no doors. Somehow the accident and her marriage had become one and the same thing, a painful problem for which there was no solution. She heard herself scream as the car rolled over and over—she saw the sky tip sideways, split in two by lightning, the leaping waves reaching out for her like some hungry monster . . . Her own screams filled her head, echoing and re-echoing.

'Abby! Abby—wake up!'

Someone was shaking her shoulder and light from the lamp on the bedside table shone into her eyes as she opened them. She stared up into troubled eyes, then a face came into focus—Marc's face. He was bending over the bed, his hair tousled from sleep. 'I'm sorry. I had to wake you. You were screaming.'

She sat up, weak with relief as the horror of the dream faded. 'I was having a nightmare,' she whispered. 'I had an accident this afternoon.'

'I know. Mrs Morelle told me.' He sat down on the edge of the bed. 'I looked in on you when I came in, but you were asleep.' He touched her shoulder. 'Are you all right—sure you weren't hurt?'

She shook her head. 'Alan came along—Alan Blake. If it hadn't been for him I don't think I'd be here now.' She looked at him, tears filling her eyes. 'Oh, Marc, I was almost killed.'

He pulled her roughly into his arms and held her close. 'It was that damned car. You should have done as I said and taken the BMW while it was being serviced.'

She shook her head despondently. 'I know—you were right. But I've been thinking. Perhaps it would have been better for you if Alan hadn't come along—if I'd—' He held her away from him and the words died in her throat at the angry look in his eyes.

'*Don't!* Don't talk like that—do you hear?'

For a moment they stared at each other. The expression in Marc's eyes changed from anger to pain, then suddenly he crushed her to him. His mouth found hers and he kissed her, hungrily—desperately. She clung to him, grateful at first for the comfort of his kiss and then, as passion and desire mounted in her, eager for his love. Her fingers tangled in his hair as she felt him gently undo the simple fastening of her nightdress. His lips were warm against her throat and shoulders as he whispered her name over and over. As his hands caressed her there was only one thought in her mind: Marc was hers after all. He did love and want her. This was her chance to prove to him that their marriage need not be a sham— that she could make him happy.

As he slipped into bed beside her she reached out for him, holding him close—giving herself completely. It was as though the rest of the world fell away. There was nothing but Marc. Their bodies in perfect harmony, they reached undreamed-of heights of ecstasy together until at last they lay still in each other's arms. Marc whispered endearments in her ear, pressing her head into the hollow of his shoulder as he stroked her hair. Abigail slept almost instantly, all her nightmares over, all her fears laid to rest, wrapped securely in the warmth of her husband's arms.

The first thing she heard was the singing of the birds. Sunlight played on her eyelids and she opened them. For once she did not dread the coming day. Slowly the events of the previous night drifted back to her and happiness flooded through her like a draught of wine. She rolled over, reaching out her hand to Marc, but his side of the bed was empty, with only a dent in the pillow to prove that he had been there—that the whole thing wasn't a dream. Languidly she rolled into his empty place, burying her face in his pillow to inhale the fragrance of his hair, drowsily reliving the delight they had found in each other last night and speculating on the difference it would make to their future. She heard the grandfather clock on the landing outside strike and counted—it was eight o'clock! She must get up or she would be late! Hurriedly she went into the bathroom, showered and dressed in her uniform, wondering where Marc could be.

As she walked through the house that morning she looked at everything with new eyes. Perhaps she should do some redecorating. She could see now that it was needed and it might be fun—something she and Marc could share. There was the dinner party she had dreaded giving, too. Now it was something to look forward to with pleasure. This morning everything looked different. She felt a completely new person. For the first time she felt like Abigail DeLisle—Marc's wife.

She was crossing the hall to go into the dining-room when the telephone rang. Picking up the receiver she said, 'Hello. DeLisle House, Mrs Marcus DeLisle speaking.'

'Good morning, Abigail. It's Lesley. I've just heard about your hair-raising accident. Are you all right?'

Abigail realised with a small shock that she had forgotten all about the accident. 'I'm fine,' she said. 'Who told you anyway?'

'Alan Blake rang me a few minutes ago.'

'Did he? Why should he do that, I wonder?' Abigail felt slightly irritated. She had, after all, asked that no fuss be made about it.

'He seemed to think you should rest today—said you'd had a bad shaking up, but that you'd made light of it.'

'Rubbish! I'm fine—never better,' Abigail said.

'I think he's right—you should take the day off. I'll arrange for someone to take your calls. That's final, Abby,' Lesley said firmly. 'I don't want to hear any arguments.'

Abigail was about to protest, then she remembered something. 'Actually, I do have the police coming this morning for a statement,' she said slowly. Lesley seized on this.

'That settles it! Have a day off. Do something completely different—put your feet up.' There was a pause, then she asked, 'Has Marc checked you over? Do you want me to come over and take a look at you?'

Abigail laughed. 'No! I didn't get a scratch—honestly. It was just the shock and the experience that was upsetting. You know, if I stay here I'll be bored stiff. I'll probably only work on the arrangements for the dinner party.'

But Lesley was not to be put off. 'All right, you have

my permission to do that—as long as I'm to be invited, that is!'

'I'll need time to think about that,' Abigail laughed. She broke off as she heard a car on the drive outside. 'Oh, I think I can hear Marc coming. I'll have to dash now—bye!' Putting the receiver down she ran to the front door and threw it open. Marc was getting out of the car, taking his case from the back seat. She ran to him.

'Marc, darling! Were you called out? I didn't hear the phone. I'm glad you're back in time for us to have breakfast together. Lesley just rang—' She stopped short as he turned to her. His face was grey and haggard and he looked desperately tired. 'Darling, what is it?'

He walked past her and up the steps without speaking. She followed him to the study, her heart sinking. In the doorway she hesitated. 'Marc, has something happened? Please—can't you tell me?'

He stood staring down at his desk for a moment, then he looked at her. 'I've just lost a patient,' he said quietly. 'It was two o'clock when I was called out. I've been with her ever since.'

She crossed the room to touch his arm. 'Marc, I'm so sorry, but it's inevitable—something we have to come to terms with in our work.'

He looked vaguely at her hand lying on his arm, then at her face. 'This time was a little different. She was my mother's best friend. Her going brought back—certain memories.'

She tried to slip her arms around him but he put her firmly from him. Looking down at her he said stiffly, 'About last night—it shouldn't have happened. I'm sorry. I'm afraid I took advantage of the situation, allowed my control to slip. It was unforgivable.'

Abigail stared at him in disbelief. His mouth was set in

a determined line and his eyes were cool—looking at her as though she were a stranger. She stepped back, her hand dropping from his arm. He started towards the door and she asked, 'What about breakfast?'

'No time. I must shave and change for surgery. I had something at the hospital.' He didn't even look at her as he spoke.

Slowly she walked into the dining-room and sat bleakly alone at the long table. Last night might have been a dream. Nothing had changed—nothing at all, except that the sun had suddenly gone in and the birds had stopped singing.

CHAPTER EIGHT

As soon as she was alone in the house Abigail regretted her decision to take the day off. Ten minutes after Marc had left for the surgery a young policeman arrived to take her statement, and after that the rest of the day stretched endlessly before her. Determined not to allow herself to brood on Marc's change of mood, she went into the kitchen to find Mrs Morelle.

'I'm planning to give a dinner party,' she told her. 'Will you help me with the menu and the guest-list, please?'

'Of course I will.' The housekeeper took a notebook and pencil from the dresser drawer. 'I'll make us some coffee first, shall I? While I'm doing it perhaps you'd like to go through the recipe books and make some choices.'

It was an enjoyable hour. At the end of it Abigail found herself with a list of invitations to write, but before she went off to do it Mrs Morelle asked, 'Did Dr Marcus have his breakfast at the hospital this morning?'

Abigail swallowed hard. 'Yes, he was rather upset at losing a patient. He said she was his mother's best friend.

Mrs Morelle sighed and shook her head. 'Ah yes, that would be Mrs Vernon. She's been ill for a long time. She wasn't young of course, but then—' She looked at Abigail. 'Was Doctor with her at the last?'

'Yes. Apparently he went to the hospital at two this morning.'

The housekeeper looked thoughtful. 'No wonder he

was upset. It will have brought back so many painful memories.'

Abigail wrote the dinner party invitations at the little writing desk in the drawing-room, then looked at her watch. It was still only eleven o'clock. What was she to do with the rest of the day? Her thoughts drifted back to Marc and the hurt stirred anew in her heart. Why had he considered last night such a mistake? Was loving her such a disaster? The sound of a car approaching brought her to her feet, glad of some diversion. From the window she saw its long red shape drawing to a smooth halt in front of the house. Alan waved to her as he uncoiled himself from the driving seat. Her heart lifted as she went to the front door. Today she needed company—someone who could make her laugh. A half-hour with Alan might lift her out of her depression a little.

He grinned and held out a large box of chocolates. 'Sweets for the sweet! I'm glad to see you looking so well after your ordeal last night. By the way, I've just been watching them removing the wreckage of your car from the bottom of the cliff.'

Abigail shuddered. 'The police have been for my statement too. But if you don't mind, I'd rather not talk about it any more.'

'Understandably—that's precisely why I'm here!' He smiled invitingly. 'Come out and have lunch with me?'

She hesitated. 'Oh—but don't you have work to do?'

'Nothing that won't improve with the keeping. Oh, come on. You know it isn't good for you, sitting here and brooding. I wouldn't mind betting you've never seen this island properly yet.'

She had to admit that he was right. From the moment of their arrival she and Marc had been up to their eyes in work.

He took her to a small, exclusive restaurant where they ate in the open, on a terrace overlooking the sea. Then they drove to St Peter Port to visit the open-air market with its gay, striped awnings. Abigail was intrigued to see ladies in the costume of a bygone age, selling home-made preserves and cakes, *gaches*—the traditional fruit-bread—and other delights, and speaking to each other in the old French patois of the island. Alan guided her through cobbled streets past sturdily built granite houses to the French *halles*, the old covered market where fresh fish and island-grown vegetables were being sold. Finally they walked down to the harbour and Abigail gazed in delight at the forest of bobbing masts on the sparkling water. Alan pointed to a smart cabin cruiser painted blue and white that was moored nearby.

'That's *Dancing Lady*—she's mine. Perhaps you'll let me take you for a trip in her one of these days?'

Abigail smiled. 'She's a beautiful boat. I'd love to go—if Marc is invited too, that is.'

He pulled a face. 'Spoil-sport! Anyway, what hope would there be of Marc taking time off? He's always too busy for anything—even his own honeymoon.' He took her hand and pulled it through his arm. 'I'll tell you one thing, Abby. If you were mine, I'd—'

She pulled her hand away. 'Alan, coming out with you today doesn't mean I'm ready to discuss my husband with you. I knew when I agreed to marry Marc that we'd have to come here and begin work right away.'

He raised an eyebrow at her. 'When you *agreed* to marry him? You make it sound like a business arrangement. But then, I suppose in a way it was!'

'That's not a very flattering thing to say,' she admonished. He picked up her hand and squeezed it.

'I assure you it wasn't meant unflatteringly.' They had reached a bench and he sat down, pulling her gently down with him, still holding her hand firmly. 'It's just that odd marriage clause in the will. A bit like something out of a Victorian novel. Some people might think it a little cold-blooded, but I'm sure Dr Stephen never intended it to be. You see, the DeLisle men have never had much luck with their women. He probably meant it as a kind of insurance—for Marc and for the DeLisle family as a whole.' He glanced at her. 'I expect you know that there have been DeLisles here since the year dot?'

She nodded. 'Yes, Marc told me. But what did you mean about them never having much luck with their women?'

He shrugged. 'It's always been there, like a kind of jinx. A history of stormy relationships and failed marriages, right up to the present generation. Dr Simon's marriage was about the most successful, but he and his wife despaired of ever having children. When at last Lesley came along she was a girl and not the son and heir they'd prayed for.'

Abigail nodded. 'I see—and of course, Marc's mother died when he was very young.'

Alan looked at her curiously. 'Well, yes—you could put it that way, I suppose.'

'What do you mean?' She turned to him.

He pulled a face. 'Well, you're right, she did die— eventually. But first she left Stephen and Marc.'

'She left them?' Abigail stared at him.

'Yes—for another man. Not many people know. Only the family's closest friends. It was all hushed up at the time. Quite a scandal in those days. Stephen refused to divorce her and she died about two years later in a car accident.'

Abigail was silent. Why hadn't Marc told her? Did he know the complete story himself? Suddenly she remembered his words to her that morning—his distress at the death of the woman who had been his mother's friend. Alan pressed her hand.

'You seem shocked. I hope I haven't spoken out of turn. After all, it's ancient history now, isn't it?'

She looked at him. 'What? Oh, yes—ancient history. Alan, the other night you said something about Marc and Lesley. I know that Marc's father didn't approve—' She stopped speaking as he winced.

'I seem to have opened my mouth a bit too wide, don't I? Forget it. It was nothing.'

'No, tell me. I have a right to know,' she insisted. 'Now that you've said so much you may as well go on.'

He looked uncomfortable. 'It really is nothing—just that they used to be pretty close, almost inseparable, you could say. When we were kids I used to get quite jealous. I always had a bit of a thing about Lesley, you see. Well, as they got older Stephen began to worry that it might get serious. It's not ideal, I suppose—first cousins.' He shrugged. 'Anyway, they both went away to study medicine and the thing died a natural death. Marc's married now to you, so that's that, isn't it?' He grinned at her, but the grin faded as he noticed her pensive expression. 'Oh look—I haven't said anything to upset you, have I?'

She turned to him coolly. 'For a solicitor you're not very tactful, are you? For all you knew I might not have known anything about that marriage clause in my father-in-law's will.'

His jaw dropped. 'Oh, my God! You did, didn't you?'

'As it happens, yes, I did,' she conceded.

He released his breath in a sigh of relief. 'Phew—you had me worried for a minute.' He smiled wryly at her. 'If you want my opinion—you probably don't, but you're going to get it anyway—I think you deserve better.' He looked into her eyes. 'You must love Marc very much.'

She swallowed hard, trying to erase the memory of the past twenty-four hours. 'If we all got what we deserve, the world would be a very different place,' she said evasively.

He nodded. 'Mmm, very profound.' He reached for her hand and stood up. 'Come on, let's go.'

In the car she suddenly remembered the dinner party invitations still in her handbag, waiting to be posted. She sorted through them and handed him his. 'Here, I almost forgot these. You might as well have yours now. It's an invitation to our first dinner party. I hope you can come.'

He slipped it out of its envelope and glanced at the date. 'As far as I know, I'm free on that date. Thanks, Abby. I'd love to come.' He turned to her, looking pleased. 'Tell you what—it's still early. Do you feel like a swim?'

She laughed at his impulsiveness. 'All right. Where?'

'The beach house—where else?' He started the car.

'I'll have to go home for my swimsuit, and to collect the key.'

He nodded. 'Right! First stop, DeLisle House!'

Abigail told Mrs Morelle where she was going, snatched a swimsuit and towel from her room and rejoined Alan in the car. On the short drive to the beach house she suddenly realised that she had enjoyed her day off after all. Alan was good company, even if he was a little too outspoken. At least he had stopped her from thinking too much.

They changed and ran down the beach together to plunge into the frothing waves. Alan was a strong swimmer but she managed to keep up with him until finally they came out to flop down on to the sand. Abigail shook the water from her hair and towelled it vigorously, then rolled on to her back to soak up the last of the late afternoon sun. Alan watched her admiringly, noticing the way the Guernsey sun had streaked her hair with gold and the honeyed glow her skin was beginning to take on. Raising himself on one elbow he studied her, eyes narrowed against the sun's glare.

'You know, this place suits you, Abby,' he said thoughtfully. 'I say "this place" because somehow I don't think marriage is doing a lot for you. There's a wistful look in your eyes.'

She sat up, hugging her knees, embarrassed by his analysis of her. 'I really don't think my marriage need concern you, Alan. Look, we've had a nice day, so why spoil it?'

'So—talking about your marriage spoils the day, does it?' he probed. 'I told you once, Abby, that if you needed a friend I'd be available.'

She turned to look at him. 'As we're being frank, Alan, I might as well tell you that you're far too indiscreet for me ever to consider you as a confidant.'

He winced. 'Ouch! I suppose I asked for that. Look, I only told you things I thought were of special concern to you. I don't go around blabbing to all and sundry, you know.'

'I'm relieved to hear it,' she told him dryly. She lay down again, closing her eyes.

For a moment he was silent, then he said, 'Marc must either be a fool or extremely sure of you.'

She opened one eye to look up at him. 'Oh?'

'Mmm. If I had a bride as lovely as you I wouldn't let her within two miles of a guy like me!'

Her lips twitched with amusement. 'I expect that's because you *are* a guy like you! It takes one to know one.'

He bent over her. 'Do you have any idea at all how damned attractive you are?' he asked. 'Do you realise that it's taking every ounce of my considerable self-control not to kiss you at this moment?'

She reached up to push at his shoulders, her heart quickening with apprehension. 'Don't be so stupid, Alan. Let me up now. It's time I was getting back.'

He didn't move. 'Can't I have just one kiss—a tiny one—for saving your life yesterday?'

'The dinner invitation will have to do for that,' she told him, vainly trying to escape from his arms planted firmly one on either side of her on the sand. 'Please, Alan, you're being very childish. Let me get up!'

But he bent, kissing her swiftly before she had a chance to turn her head away. He released her immediately and she sat up, her cheeks flaming. 'Take me home at once! If I'd known you'd behave like that I'd—' As she had been speaking she turned, getting to her feet, but she suddenly stopped, freezing in mid-movement as she saw that someone was watching them from the steps of the beach house. Even though the sun was shining in her eyes, Marc's tall figure was quite unmistakable. Alan followed her gaze and whistled softly.

'I wonder how long he's been there? Sorry, Abby. Still, I may have done you a favour at that! Maybe he'll appreciate you more now!'

'Oh!' She chewed her lip in anguish. 'You really are maddening, Alan! I hope you've got a good explanation ready for your action.'

Unperturbed, Alan got lazily to his feet. 'I've never yet needed an excuse for kissing a pretty girl—especially a married one.' He grinned at her. 'Haven't you ever heard of forbidden fruit?'

She hardly heard him. She was running up the beach to where Marc stood. As she came up to him she saw that he was angry. His mouth was set in the familiar tightly-controlled line and his eyes were dark. She was breathless as she reached him.

'Marc, Alan took me out to lunch, then we came down here for a swim. Lesley rang you see—she insisted that I took the day off.'

He stared at her stonily. 'I'm glad to see that you've made such a miraculous recovery—obviously Alan has helped you to forget your ordeal.'

She bit her lip. 'Yes, he took me to the market in St Peter Port. I had a nice day.' She trailed off, wondering whether he had actually seen Alan kiss her—whether it had looked as though she were encouraging him. She knew her cheeks were flaming—that she must look guilty. But his eyes left her, looking over her shoulder to where Alan was making his leisurely way up the beach. He had slipped on his shorts and T-shirt and wore a maddeningly smug expression. Marc's eyes moved back to Abigail's face.

'Lesley's idea was that you should take it easy for the day,' he said. 'Not go rushing about like a day-tripper!'

As Alan came up to them he raised a hand and called, 'Hello, Marc! I've been showing Abby round—hope you've no objections. Why don't you change and have a swim yourself? You look as though you could do with winding down a little.'

Abigail saw a muscle in Marc's cheek twitch at Alan's insolence, but his voice was level as he said, 'No time, I'm afraid. I have a practice meeting this evening. That's why I'm here, to look for Abigail. I've asked Mrs Morelle to serve dinner early.'

'I see. I'll be off then.' Alan laid a hand on Abigail's shoulder. 'Thank you for your company today, love— and for the invitation. I shall look forward to that. Bye then, Marc.' And, flinging his towel over his shoulder, he made off towards his car.

Marc looked at her. 'What did he mean—"Thanks for the invitation"?'

'I've been planning a dinner party,' she told him. 'I wrote the invitations this morning so I gave Alan his personally.'

'I see. It didn't occur to you to ask me first?'

She stared at him. 'I asked the people I imagined were your friends. No, I didn't think I needed your permission.'

His nostrils flared. 'I do like to have *some* say about the people who sit at my table,' he told her stiffly. 'And in future I'd prefer it if you didn't encourage Alan Blake. He has a reputation with women. How do you think it will look if you're seen around with him?'

'I doubt very much whether many people know who I am anyway,' she said pointedly. 'We haven't been seen together much, have we?' She folded her arms around herself, feeling suddenly cold. 'And now I'd like to change, if you don't mind.' He stood aside and she walked past him into the beach house, trembling half with anger and half with unhappiness. In spite of the tenderness he had shown her last night, they seemed further apart than ever. Each day that passed seemed to widen the rift between them.

In the house she dragged on her clothes, then rejoined him. He was silent on the short journey back. Once home he made for the bedroom to change before dinner, and sitting on the bed Abigail listened to the sound of the shower and wondered helplessly what to do. Should she force a showdown—tell him how intolerable her life was, demand to be set free? But supposing he agreed? However painful, she had to face the fact that being free of Marc was the last thing she wanted. She would never be able to free herself from loving him, even though a whole world separated them.

Slowly she undressed and slipped into her bathrobe. The door to the dressing-room was open and she saw him come through from the bathroom. His hair was wet and he wore a towel draped round his waist. She got up and went across to the open door.

'Marc.'

He turned to look at her.

'We have to talk. I want to know where I stand.' She took a deep breath. 'I thought—you made me believe that you loved me when you asked me to marry you. It was, naturally, a shock to discover that clause in your father's will. You must surely admit that you should have told me about it. I just don't know where I stand in all this.' She looked down at her feet to hide the colour that sprang to her cheeks. 'Especially after—after last night.'

Marc's eyes flashed dangerously. 'That didn't seem to get in the way of your obvious enjoyment of Blake's company this afternoon,' he said sarcastically. 'I told you this morning—last night was a slip on my part, a mistake. I've apologised for it. Don't think you can use it as a weapon against me!'

She took a step backwards, stung by the bitterness of his tone. 'I had no intention of doing that, and it wasn't the way it looked this afternoon. Alan was being stupid—fooling around and—' He turned abruptly from her and began to dress.

'Spare me the details. I've had a bad day, and it isn't finished yet. I'd rather not have a row, if you don't mind.'

Her patience snapped. 'I'm not trying to have a row,' she said, her voice rising. 'I'm trying to have a civilised discussion!'

'And this is neither the time nor the place!' He glared coldly at her. 'Look, obviously you feel you owe Blake something for rescuing you so gallantly yesterday, but I must insist on one thing—if you're going to have an affair with him, will you please pay me the courtesy of being discreet. I do have a certain status in King's Rock. Even if *you* don't care about that, I do!'

Her eyes blazed at him. 'I'm beginning to think that's all you do care about!' she flung at him. 'There's a theory that you never know a man until you live with him, and I've learned the truth of that since I've been here. If your father was as cold and arrogant as you, no wonder your—' She had been about to say something about his mother, but she was interrupted by a loud knocking on the bedroom door. Mrs Morelle's voice called out,

'It's the telephone for Mrs Marcus—a patient. Mr Grainger from Moulin Farm. He says his wife's pains have started. Do you want to speak to him or shall I tell him you're on your way?'

Abigail was truly grateful for the housekeeper's timely interruption. She had been about to say something she would certainly have been sorry for. It was unusual for her to lose her temper and her heart was still pounding uncomfortably as she replied, 'Just tell him I'll be there as soon as I can, Mrs Morelle.' Her eyes still on Marc, she took a step towards him. 'It's their first baby.

They're bound to be anxious. I'd better go right away. When you go down will you ask Mrs Morelle to put something in the oven for me?'

She searched his eyes, looking for a spark of warmth. She still could not believe that the man who had held her so tenderly last night, soothing away her fears, and later making such passionate love to her, could now be so cold, so cruelly indifferent.

'Of course.' He went towards the door. 'I may be gone by the time you get back. I probably shan't see you until morning.' At the door he turned, his eyes flicking over her. 'Hadn't you better get dressed?'

She looked down, suddenly aware that she was still in her bathrobe. 'Oh, yes. Marc—'

He turned in the act of opening the door. 'Yes?'

'About the dinner party—you'd better see the list before I post the rest of the invitations.'

He waved his hand dismissively. 'Leave it as it is. I realise it'll be something of an ordeal for you. It's good of you to give it.' He looked at her, his eyes enigmatic. 'Perhaps you don't think it now, Abby, but the time will soon pass—for both of us.'

She stared at the closed door, tears welling up in her eyes. For her it would be the longest year she was ever likely to live.

Jill Grainger had decided that she wanted to have her first baby at home. She and her husband ran a small farm about two miles out of King's Rock and although this was her first child, Lesley had agreed to a home confinement on the grounds that Jill was strong and fit. When Abigail arrived at the neat stone farmhouse she found Jill in the kitchen with the washing machine going. She put her head round the door.

'Hello. I thought you were supposed to be in labour?'

Jill straightened her back. 'I am. But I thought I'd better catch up on this lot before John's mother gets here tomorrow. Can't leave it all to her.' She winced, clenching her teeth as a spasm of pain gripped her. Abigail glanced at her fob watch, noting the time.

'How long have you been getting them like that?'

'Since lunch-time—though at first they were nothing much. Not much fun now though.' She sat down, her lower lip caught between her teeth. 'Good job the washing's nearly finished, isn't it?'

David Grainger put his head round the door. 'Good evening, Nurse. You'll think I'm an inconsiderate wretch, letting Jill do the washing when she's in labour, but I'd like to see anyone try and stop her!'

Abigail laughed. 'I know what you mean. But I think she'll allow you to finish it for her now while I take her off upstairs to rest. It could be a long night, you know, Jill.'

After she had checked to make sure that Jill's labour was progressing normally, Abigail went downstairs again. Standing in the kitchen, she took off her apron and rolled down her sleeves.

'Let her rest for as long as she can,' she told David, who was rolling the washing machine away under the worktop. 'Everything will be fine, I'm sure, but it will be a while yet before she goes into the second stage. I'm going home now to get a bite to eat. You can ring me there if you're at all worried about anything. I'll ring Dr Lesley and I'll be back in a couple of hours—right?'

He nodded. 'Right. I'm not new to this, you know,' he told her cheerfully. 'I always deliver the calves myself, so I'd know what to do if the worst came to the worst.'

Abigail laughed. 'It won't! But thanks for the reassurance!'

He looked out of the window to where her shiny blue BMW stood parked in the yard. 'I like your new car, Nurse. Beats that clapped out old Mini, eh?'

She pulled a face. 'I'm afraid I wrote that off yesterday,' she told him. 'Entirely my own fault. Everyone had been telling me to have it checked over for ages but I didn't make the time. The car finished up at the bottom of the cliff.'

He stared at her, aghast. 'Good God! What about you—are you all right?'

She nodded. 'I was lucky—managed to scramble out before it toppled over. It wasn't an experience I'd care to repeat though.'

He shook his head. 'You'll have to take it easy in future.' He grinned at her. 'You're getting to be pretty indispensable here, you know.'

'No one's indispensable, David,' she told him as she opened the back door. As she climbed into the car she told herself that last remark was one that applied all too painfully in her case.

Marc had already left for his meeting when she got back to the house. She ate the food that Mrs Morelle had left warming for her, then telephoned Lesley.

'I thought you'd like to know that Jill Grainger has gone into labour,' she said. 'It's three days before her expected date, but everything seems to be going well.'

'All the same, I think I'd like to be present for the birth,' Lesley said. 'I really prefer first babies to be born in hospital, as you know. Have you taken all the necessary equipment out to her?'

'Yes. I took the gas and air cylinders earlier. Everything's organised. Anyway, I thought you were having a practice meeting this evening?' Abigail was slightly piqued that she wasn't allowed to deliver without supervision, but she tried not to let it creep into her voice.

'We are having a meeting,' Lesley said. 'But naturally patients come first. Anyway, we'll probably be through by the time I'm needed.'

'I still don't think there's any need,' Abigail told her. 'David Grainger insists that he could deliver the baby himself if the worst came to the worst. He says he's used to being midwife to his cows!'

Lesley laughed. 'Well, if he bestows one quarter of the attention to his wife as he does to that herd of Guernseys of his, she's on to a winner! Give me a ring when she goes into the second stage, will you, Abby? See you at Moulin Farm later then. Oh, by the way, did you have a nice day off?'

'Fine, thanks.'

'Did you see anything of Alan? He said he might look in on you—maybe take you out for lunch.'

'Yes, he did. It was good of him to think of it.' As she put the telephone down, it occurred to Abigail for the first time that the day's outing with Alan might have been engineered by Lesley herself. She always seemed friendly enough, but she must be eager to have her out of the way. Abigail stood by the telephone table, remembering the scrap of conversation between Lesley and Marc, overheard at the beach house on the night of the barbecue. But her thoughts were cut off abruptly by the telephone ringing again at her elbow. Startled, she picked up the receiver quickly. Could Jill's labour have accelerated? But it wasn't David Grainger at the other end of the line—she was in for a surprise.

'Hello—Abby? Jennifer here. I've been trying to get

you for ages. First there was no reply, then your line was engaged.'

'Jennifer! How lovely to hear you. Yes, I have been busy this evening,' she explained. 'I've got a mother in labour at the moment.'

'So you're still nursing? Well, I don't blame you. How are you, darling? How is married bliss?'

'Great! Just great.' Abigail hoped that she didn't sound over-bright. 'But I thought you were still in America?'

'I managed to get away a week earlier. To tell you the truth, I got homesick. Can you imagine it? *Me*—homesick! Anyway, the upshot is that I've got a few spare days' holiday due to me now, and I wondered if I might come over and meet this new son-in-law of mine?'

Abigail knew a moment of sheer panic. There would be no pulling the wool over Jennifer's eyes. She was much too shrewd not to notice that all was not well between them—yet how could she put her off? 'Oh! But of course. I shall look forward to seeing you very much,' she said. 'When were you thinking of coming?'

There was a pause, then Jennifer said, 'Did I detect a slight hesitation? If it isn't convenient, just say. I can make it some other time.'

'No! Of course you must come. I'd love you to. It's just that I'd planned to have some redecoration done before your visit—that's all. When can we expect you?'

'In a couple of weeks' time. When I've had time to sort things out at the office and do some reorganising.'

'Oh, that's fine. We have a dinner party planned. You'll enjoy that. It's rather a quiet life we live here, you know.'

Jennifer's voice was amused as she said, 'I'm coming to see you, you know. Don't worry about entertaining me. After the pace of life in America I shall be grateful for a bit of peace and quiet. And now I'd better get off the phone so that you can get on with your vital work. I'll let you know the time of my plane and everything. Bye, darling.'

'I know you're tired, Jill, but it won't be long now. The baby's head is clearly visible.' Lesley's forehead was beaded with perspiration as she leaned over her patient. 'Please try hard for me once more—please.'

Jill rolled her head from side to side on the pillow. 'I can't—I can't do it any more. I want to go to sleep.'

Lesley looked at Abigail, her eyes anxious over her mask. They both knew that Jill was exhausted. The second stage of labour had lasted much longer than either of them had anticipated and Abigail knew that Lesley was wishing she had insisted that the Grainger baby be born in hospital. Lesley took David's arm and drew him to one side, out of his wife's hearing.

'Can you try to encourage her, David? I'd really prefer not to use the forceps.'

His face was anxious. 'Everything is all right, isn't it, Doctor?'

Lesley nodded. 'So far, yes, but it's high time the baby was born. I don't have to tell you that, do I? I know she's tired but if you can urge her to try just that bit harder next time there is a pain . . . It'll come so much better from you.' Returning to Abigail, she said quietly, 'I'm going to perform an episiotomy with the next contraction. I'll use the anaesthetic spray. It'll be better than nothing, but I do wish we'd had her in hospital. We could have done an epidural.'

They waited anxiously, David speaking softly to his wife, holding her hand and talking to her about the baby, reminding her of the names they had chosen and all the plans they had made. The next contraction came and he lifted her shoulders up and forward. Lesley performed a neat episiotomy, explaining briefly to her patient what she was doing and why. A few moments later the baby was born. After satisfying herself that all was well, Lesley stood aside and allowed Abigail to take over— tying and severing the cord and handing the baby to David to hold until the third stage was complete.

'A boy, Jill!' he told his wife proudly. 'A son to carry on the farm. And he's a great-looking lad—even if he does look as if he's been in a fight!'

Lesley came back to suture the episiotomy, then peeled off her gloves and mask with a sigh. 'I'll leave the rest to you, Nurse,' she told Abigail. She smiled at David. 'Do you mind if I go down and put the kettle on? I think we could all do with a strong cup of tea.'

'Help yourself, Doc,' he grinned. 'Tonight you can have anything in the house—except these two, that is!'

When the newest addition to the Grainger household was asleep in his cot and Jill was bathed and comfortable, they left the new parents to drink their tea together, taking theirs in the kitchen downstairs. Lesley heaved a sigh of relief.

'Thank God that's over! In future I'm having no nonsense about first babies being born at home. They'll be delivered in hospital, even if it's a short-stay job.' She glanced at Abigail over the rim of her cup. 'You're looking a bit peaky—still suffering from the reaction to your accident?'

Abigail smiled wanly. 'I suppose you could call it that.' She looked at Lesley. 'Was it your idea that Alan should take me out to lunch today, by the way?'

Lesley looked surprised. '*Mine?* Hardly! The day I

have to prompt Alan to ask an attractive female out to lunch I'll know he's losing his touch!'

Abigail stirred her tea thoughtfully. 'Marc wasn't very happy about our spending the day together. I thought you might have known his feelings on the subject as you and he are so close.' She looked up in time to catch the flush of colour in Lesley's cheeks.

'What are you trying to say, Abby?' she asked quietly.

Abigail shook her head. 'I'm not sure. I do know that there's more between the two of you than I've been led to believe. Alan told me—'

'Alan is an inveterate gossip. You can write off anything he might have told you as pure conjecture!' Lesley said hotly.

Abigail looked up at her calmly. 'They do say there's no smoke without fire, don't they? On the night of the barbecue I overheard you advising Marc about something you said I had a right to know. Perhaps *you* should tell me.'

The colour left Lesley's face. She opened her mouth to speak, but at that moment David came into the kitchen.

'Fell asleep!' he announced with a smile. 'Right slap in the middle of a sentence! But I reckon she deserves a good rest, bless her. You too—both of you. You did a great job. I can't thank you enough.'

Lesley got up from the table and began to put on her coat and gather up her case. 'I'll look in in the morning, David—just to make sure everything is all right. Better get some rest yourself now. You did well. I don't know what we'd have done without you, eh, Nurse?'

Abigail smiled as she buttoned her own coat. 'I certainly don't. You can give yourself a pat on the back. See you in the morning, David.'

Out in the yard Lesley lost no time. Before Abigail had time to reach her own car she heard the familiar buzz of the 'biscuit tin's' engine and saw the red tail-lights of Lesley's car as they disappeared out through the farm gates. Obviously she had no intention of pursuing the line of conversation Abigail had started over the teacups!

CHAPTER NINE

JILL GRAINGER made a speedy recovery from her difficult confinement and her little son was soon thriving. After the night of his birth Abigail did not speak to Lesley again about her relationship with Marc. Her accident was forgotten and she saw no more of Alan; not that that was difficult with all she had to do. There was a sudden spate of births in King's Rock which kept her busy, while at home she tried to do as much as she could to get ready for her mother's visit as well as the impending dinner party. After the way Marc had objected to her making a guest list without consulting him, she was a little apprehensive about telling him of her mother's visit, but she need not have worried. She broke the news to him at breakfast on the morning after the Grainger baby's birth.

'Mind? Of course I don't mind,' he had said, looking up at her in surprise across the table. 'While you're here this is your home—you're entitled to invite your mother.'

The 'while you're here' had not escaped her notice. 'I didn't really see how I could refuse when she asked to come,' she explained. 'And as she wasn't able to be at the wedding she's naturally anxious to meet you. I know it's awkward but—'

He looked at her with a slight lift of an eyebrow. 'I take it you haven't told her that our circumstances are—unusual?'

She looked down at her plate. 'No.'

'Do you intend to?'

She looked up, meeting his eyes. 'No. Jennifer and I have never been close. I've never been in the habit of running to her with all my problems. Anyway, our marriage is no one's business but our own, isn't it?'

He shrugged as he rose from the table, apparently content to leave it at that, but as the day of Jennifer's arrival drew near Abigail could not help the feeling of apprehension that nagged at her. Would Marc go along with her deception? Would he play the part of the attentive husband as enthusiastically as he had for his own friends, or would he feel it was unnecessary to put on an act for a woman he might never meet again?

On the afternoon before her mother was due, Abigail was working at the ante-natal clinic with Lesley. It was a hot, humid day and they were short-staffed because of the holiday season. As the hours went by she grew weary. The queue of patients seemed endless and most of them seemed to have bored, fractious toddlers in tow. Suddenly the clinic seemed unbearably hot and airless and the noise almost intolerable. Once or twice Lesley looked at her curiously.

'Are you all right?' she asked between patients as Abigail changed the disposable sheet on the examination couch and checked the trolley. She glanced up, her face pale, murmuring that she was fine.

The last patient came in, looking flushed and muttering about the heat and the length of time she had been waiting. She had come for her post-natal examination and had brought her six-week-old baby with her as well as his two-year-old brother. Abigail gave the baby to one of the voluntary helpers to look after and weighed the patient, then took her blood pressure, noting the results before ushering her in to Lesley's room for her examination and cervical smear test. She had tried to persuade the little boy to go into the crèche and play with the toys there, but he was fretful, clinging to his mother's hand and refusing to leave her. As she was the last patient of the afternoon, Abigail took his hand herself and tried to find something which would divert his attention, but he squirmed and twisted away from her, running round the room and knocking a pile of books and magazines to the floor. She caught up with him and grasped him round the waist.

'Come and sit down with me until Mummy is ready,' she begged, holding his wriggling body and trying to pick up the books at the same time. Suddenly he was sick— violently and copiously sick—over the books, himself and Abigail. Tears pricked her eyelids. It seemed the last straw. Mrs Davis, the last of the voluntary helpers, who had been about to leave, rushed to her assistance with a cloth and a bowl of disinfectant.

'Oh dear, oh dear,' she muttered sympathetically. 'It's the heat and the long wait. This is no place for small children really—but what can you do if you've no one to leave them with?' She glanced at Abigail's chalk-white face and exclaimed, 'Are you feeling all right, Nurse DeLisle? You've gone very pale.'

Abigail rose unsteadily to her feet, the room spinning round her. She made a hasty dash for the cloakroom, getting there only just in time.

Ten minutes later she stood leaning her head wearily against the cool tiles, her head aching and her skin cold and clammy. She couldn't remember feeling like this before. Queasiness was not a problem with her and never had been. During her training the delicacy of her stomach had been tested to the full, so why should a small child being sick have made her react like this? Taking a deep breath, she tottered back to the waiting room and sat down on one of the chairs. The place was empty now and Mrs Davis was putting on her coat.

'Feel better now, dear?' she asked sympathetically. 'Dr Lesley is making you a cup of tea. Is there anything I can do for you before I go?'

Abigail shook her head. 'No, thank you. I'll be fine now. It must have been something I ate for lunch.'

The woman left and a moment later Lesley appeared with a tray of tea. She peered anxiously at Abigail. 'Mrs Davis told me you weren't feeling well so I thought we'd have a cup of tea before we leave. I could do with a breather too.' She put the tray down on a low table and seated herself opposite Abigail. 'How do you feel now?'

Abigail managed a smile. 'Better thanks. I think it must have been something I ate—and the weather hasn't helped. It's so hot.'

'Have you been sick?' Lesley laid a cool hand on her brow and lifted her wrist, feeling for the pulse. 'Look, when you've had this drink I'm taking you home. Someone can come and collect your car later. And I'm going to insist that you take a few days off.'

'But I'm all right now—honestly,' Abigail protested weakly. 'It was just the heat. When that child was sick I somehow—' But Lesley wasn't listening.

'You've got your mother coming, haven't you? Then there's the dinner party. You've been working very hard. You can do with a break. You and Marc didn't even have a honeymoon. Look—oh dear, have I said something?'

Tears were coursing helplessly down Abigail's cheeks. Acutely embarrassed, she fumbled for a handkerchief.

'I'm sorry,' she muttered. 'I don't know what's the matter with me today.'

'I do. You're run down,' Lesley said firmly, 'Come along now, drink that tea and then we're going home. And don't give me any more arguments!'

Outside in the car park Abigail insisted that she was fit to drive herself home. Lesley still looked doubtful.

'Are you really sure? You don't want another accident, do you?'

'I'm sure. I really do feel quite normal again now.' Abigail laid a hand on Lesley's arm. 'I'd rather you didn't mention this to Marc, by the way.'

Once more Lesley looked at her curiously. 'Look, Abby, why not pop into the surgery one night next week and let me check you over?'

Abigail forced a laugh as she unlocked the door of the BMW. 'You doctors are all alike! I never dared tell my father if I didn't feel a hundred per cent. Before I knew it he'd be turning me inside out! I notice you're not so thorough when it comes to looking after yourselves though!' She waved from the car window and Leslie called,

'All right—but don't forget what I said. Take a long weekend. Have a good rest.'

The following day dawned bright and clear, a fine haze over the sea promising more hot weather. Abigail dressed in a cool green linen suit to go to the airport to meet Jennifer, feeling her heart lift at the prospect of seeing her mother and taking a few days off.

Jennifer looked elegant as she stepped off the plane. She wore a plain cream silk suit and her blonde hair had been cut in a smart new style which made her look younger than ever. Abigail hugged her warmly.

'You look marvellous! Oh, Jennifer, it's so lovely to

see you. Shall we have a coffee before I drive you back to King's Rock?'

Over the coffee Jennifer eyed her daughter shrewdly. There was a subtle change in her, but apart from the fact that she looked downright peaky she couldn't put a finger on it. Accepting a second cup she said, 'I expected to see you looking fit and brown as the proverbial berry, but you don't look as though you've been taking advantage of all this sunshine. You've lost weight too. Are you all right, darling?'

Abigail laughed. 'I'm fine—never better, though it's true that we've been busy. All the expected babies seemed to arrive over the same few days. The last couple of weeks have been really hectic.'

Jennifer frowned. 'What did they do before *you* arrived on the island?'

'I'm not saying that *I* did all the work,' Abigail put in quickly. 'As a matter of fact Dr Lesley—Marc's cousin, who is the doctor I work with—insisted that I should take this weekend off so that I could spend the time with you.'

Jennifer smiled wryly. 'That was big of him!'

'Her,' Abigail corrected. 'Lesley is a woman doctor—and a very good one too. She's hoping to specialise in obstetrics eventually.'

'You don't work with your husband, then?'

Abigail shook her head. 'No—you see, in order to give Lesley the experience she needs, her father and Marc let her take all the obstetric cases. Clinics and so on.'

Jennifer regarded her for a moment, then said perceptively, 'I see—so you don't see much of him, one way and another?'

Abigail picked up her handbag and Jennifer's small

overnight case, busying herself to hide the tell-tale flush she knew was staining her cheeks. 'No. Shall we go and collect the rest of your luggage now? By the time we've driven back to King's Rock it will be lunch-time, and I don't like to keep Mrs Morelle waiting.'

So that her mother wouldn't prove too much, Abigail kept up a steady flow of chatter all the way back to King's Rock, pointing out places of interest and promising to take her mother on a sight-seeing tour during her stay. When at last they drove in through the gates of DeLisle House Jennifer's eyes widened and she gave a low whistle.

'Phew! What a heavenly place! I'd no idea it would be as grand as this. Aren't you tempted to give up nursing and become the lady of the manor?'

Abigail shook her head. 'Oh no. Mrs Morelle looks after the place better than I ever could. When you meet her and taste her cooking you'll agree with me. I feel I'm better employed at doing the thing I've been trained for.'

Jennifer made no reply as she got out of the car to help with the cases, but she continued to watch her daughter shrewdly, noting her quick, nervous movements and the two bright spots of colour that burned in her cheeks— that subtle something in her eyes that she could not quite define.

First Abigail took her mother to the kitchen to intro-duce her to Mrs Morelle, then she took her on a tour of the house. One of the first things that took Jennifer's eye was the portrait of Pierre DeLisle at the top of the stairs.

'What a fascinating-looking man. Who was he?' she asked.

'Marc's wicked ancestor,' Abigail told her. 'He was the first settler here. A pirate—the genuine article. He took the place by storm—pillaging, raping, the lot! But the family became respectable again during the French Revolution when they opened their doors to refugee aristocrats.'

Jennifer stared at her. '*Well!* I'd no idea you'd married into such a colourful family! Now I feel almost nervous of meeting this Marc of yours.'

'Oh, they're all reformed characters now,' Abigail laughed. 'You've no need to worry.'

She showed Jennifer to her room, then went to her own to change. Closing the door, she sat on the bed with a sigh. How was she to keep up this show of light-heartedness throughout the coming days? In one way she would have been better off at work, though she had to admit that she was glad of the rest.

Marc and Jennifer seemed to take to each other on sight. Marc was charming and Abigail was grateful for the way he welcomed her mother—even making a point of coming in to lunch especially to meet her. She felt sure that even Jennifer could find no fault in the attentive way he behaved towards her and by the time they went out that afternoon she was feeling much more at ease. Inevitably the conversation turned to Marc once they were in the car.

'He's very good-looking,' Jennifer remarked. 'Even more so than he appeared in the wedding photographs you sent me.' She turned to her daughter. 'You *are* happy, aren't you, darling?'

Abigail kept her eyes on the road ahead. 'Of course,' she said brightly. 'Guernsey is a fantastic place. I'm so lucky.'

She took Jennifer to St Peter Port and showed her the colourful markets and quaint cobbled streets, ending up at the harbour where they sat in the sunshine watching the boats and the throng of holiday makers. Suddenly a voice hailed them.

'Hi there, stranger!'

Almost before Abigail could turn to see who it was, Alan Blake's hand came down on her shoulder. He wore shorts and a T-shirt and looked bronzed and handsome as he bent to kiss her. 'Well, how are you, love? Still helping the population to explode?'

Abigail coloured at his enthusiastic welcome. 'Alan— what a surprise! I'm having a few days off. I'd like you to meet my mother. Jennifer, this is Alan Blake, Marc's solicitor's son.'

Alan gazed at Jennifer admiringly. 'Well—if I didn't know you better I'd say you were putting me on! I can certainly see now where Abby gets her looks!' He sat down next to them. 'Are you staying long?'

'Only for a couple of days, I'm afraid,' Jennifer told him. 'I've never been to the Channel Islands before and I'm beginning to realise what I've missed.'

'You haven't lived if you haven't seen our wonderful island!' Alan said. 'We shall have to do something about it without delay. I'm having a day on the boat. How about letting me take you both for a trip?' He looked from one to the other hopefully, but Abigail looked doubtful.

'We're hardly dressed for crewing, Alan.'

He looked outraged. '*Crewing?* Do you really think I'd allow two such gorgeous creatures to *crew* for me? All you'd be required to do would be to lie on deck and give me something beautiful to look at!' His eyes twinkled wickedly at them. 'And if you've brought your bikinis with you, all the better!'

Abigail looked at her mother. 'Well—it's up to you really. It's your holiday.'

Jennifer smiled. 'It sounds lovely. I'd like to go very much.'

Alan slapped his thigh. 'Great! We can have tea on board too. I've everything laid on in the galley.'

As he led the way to the boat, Jennifer smiled at Abigail. 'Quite a smoothie,' she whispered. 'But very charming.'

It was a pleasant afternoon. They sailed northwards to round the island at its topmost point. Alan showed them L'Ancresse where the windsurfing school had its home in the deep, sheltered bay and pointed out the Beaucette Yacht Marina. The sea was smooth with only a slight swell to rock the scattered crafts with their white sails. A light haze lay over the water and from the sea the island looked green and truly beautiful. Jennifer repeated the names of the places that Alan pointed out.

'Meillette Bay—Cocagne—La Fontenelle. They sound so romantic,' she said dreamily. 'You really are lucky, Abby. This place is sheer heaven. I shan't want to go back to London when the time comes, I can see that already!'

Alan looked across at Abigail. 'All right? Not feeling seasick at all?'

Puzzled, she shook her head. 'Not at all—why, should I?'

'No—it was only that Lesley mentioned that you'd been a bit under the weather lately. I thought the boat might—'

Abigail got to her feet hurriedly, her cheeks warm with colour. 'I do wish people would stop taking such an interest in my welfare,' she said crossly. 'I simply ate something that disagreed with me, that's all. I'll go and make the tea, shall I? No, don't worry, I'll find the things.'

In the tiny galley she bit her lip. Why must Lesley tell Alan everything when she said herself that he was an inveterate gossip? He *would* have to mention it in front of Jennifer, too.

Alan switched off the engine and they floated lazily while they ate their tea on the deck of the little cruiser. Abigail had found chocolate biscuits and a Swiss roll in the cupboard below deck and she remarked on Alan's preparedness. His eyes twinkled as he replied, 'Ah—we spiders always have to keep our webs well baited, you know. I usually manage to find a shipmate when I take the *Lady* out.'

Jennifer looked at him speculatively over the rim of her cup. 'I'm not surprised—except to wonder why there isn't a permanent "mate" on board.'

To Abigail's surprise Alan's colour heightened. As he reached out to help himself to another slice of cake he said, 'The right candidate for the job hasn't come along yet. At least, she has, but she doesn't seem interested in applying.'

Jennifer made no reply, but when she and Abigail were on their way home in the car she glanced at her daughter.

'Is that young man in love with you?'

Startled, Abigail took her eyes off the road to stare at her. 'Good heavens no! He just likes to fool around. Frankly, I don't think Alan's capable of loving anyone except himself.'

Jennifer looked thoughtful. 'Mmm—don't let that suave manner deceive you. Unless I'm very much mistaken he's eating his heart out over some girl. If it isn't you, I wonder who it is?'

The following day Abigail took her mother to the beach house and they spent the morning and early afternoon swimming and sunbathing. They ate the picnic lunch packed for them by Mrs Morelle and when they had finished Jennifer lay back on her lounger with a sigh.

Ah—this is the life. I envy you, Abby. A handsome husband, a beautiful home on this gorgeous island, amusing friends, to say nothing of a career you love—' She opened her half-closed eyes and turned to look directly at Abigail. 'Which brings me to the sixty-five thousand dollar question—why are you so unhappy?'

Taken off-guard, Abigail coloured hotly. 'What on earth makes you ask that? Of course I'm happy.' She rose and began to collect the picnic things together, hastily pushing them into the basket. 'I'm going up to the beach house now to change, then I'm going up to give Morrie a hand with the preparations for tonight,' she announced. 'It isn't fair to leave it all to her. You stay here. I'll leave the car for you and walk up. It isn't far if I take the cliff path.' Before Jennifer could reply she ran up the beach to change, but when she came out of the beach house bathroom her mother was waiting for her, a look of concern on her face.

'Abby—I'm sorry. I've upset you. I didn't mean to pry, but if there's anything you want to talk about—'

'There isn't!' Abigail frowned and put out a hand to touch her mother's arm. 'Sorry. I didn't mean to snap. I don't think talking would help. Don't worry about me, Jennifer. I'll work it out.' And before the subject could be probed further she hurried out of the house, heading for the cliff path.

The dining-room at DeLisle House looked elegant. The silverware on the long table gleamed in the light from the tall red candles. Abigail had laid it with the cloth of old

Brussels lace that had been Marcus's grandmother's and she had picked flowers from the garden and arranged them herself—red roses and delicate sprays of gypsophila. When she had made sure that everything was under control and Mrs Morelle did not need any help, she went upstairs to change.

In her room she stared at her pale reflection in the mirror. Although she had acquired a light, golden tan, her skin had a luminous pallor that no amount of make-up could disguise. She had bought a new dress for the party and now she took it out of the wardrobe and held it against herself. It was made of a soft floating material in her favourite shade of blue—like a summer evening sky. The neckline was deeply cut and gently ruffled and the sleeves floated, cape-like, to her elbows. She slipped into the silky underslip that went with it, reaching to zip it at the back, then sat down at the dressing-table to do her face and hair. She heard the door of the dressing-room close. Marc had arrived to get ready. Her heart quickened. Should she speak to him? She needed his support tonight. Although he always behaved impeccably in public, she needed to be reassured that they were at least friends. She slipped on her dress and went to the connecting door.

'Marc.'

As she opened it he turned in the act of taking off his jacket. 'Hello. I came as soon as I could. It's been quite a day one way and another. Everyone seems to choose today to be ill! The evening surgery was packed—you'd think people would know not to lie in the sun for hours on end, wouldn't you?' He looked at his watch. 'Half an hour. I'll just have time for a quick bath.' He glanced at her. 'Sorry—did you want something?'

She went to him. 'Just to say thank you for being so

nice to Jennifer,' she said haltingly. 'I know you've made a special effort and I appreciate it.'

He smiled. 'Not at all. She's a very nice woman. It isn't difficult to get along with her.'

They looked at each other in silence for a moment, then he asked, 'Was that all?'

'I—oh, I wondered—I can't quite reach the top of my zip—could you?' She turned. His fingers on her skin made her tremble as he closed the top few inches of the zip. She turned, looking up at him, her eyes silently pleading.

'Marc, I—'

He touched her hair, his eyes softening as they took in her appearance. The sapphire blue dress set off her pallor, giving her an ethereal quality. 'You're looking very lovely tonight, Abby,' he said softly. He reached out to stroke her cheek with one finger. 'You're pale though. I hope—'

'Marc.' She caught his hand at the wrist. 'Marc, I've been meaning to talk to you—there's something—' He cut off her words with a shake of his head.

'Abby—have you seen the time?' He turned towards the bathroom, unbuttoning his shirt. 'We'll talk later. Our guests will be arriving soon. I don't want to be half-dressed when they do.'

With a sigh she wandered back to her room. Of course he was right. Perhaps later when the guests had gone home—when there was more time to think out what to say.

She received the guests serenely, confident that the evening would be a success. Mrs Morelle had cooked a meal fit for royalty. Asparagus from the garden as a starter; tender chicken cooked in a sauce made with herbs and wine, garnished with young vegetables, followed by a choice of three sumptuous sweets. Jennifer looked beautiful in a black dress, her blonde hair shining and her skin glowing with its newly-acquired tan. She seemed to take at once to Simon and Lesley, who were the first to arrive. They were all having a pre-dinner drink in the drawing-room when Mrs Morelle put her head round the door.

'Telephone—for you, Dr Marcus.'

He put down his glass with a sigh and looked round apologetically. 'Oh dear. I hope this isn't what I think it is!' Abigail and Jennifer exchanged glances.

Marc's worst fears were confirmed. He was called out to a patient who had had a severe coronary. He did not return. Abigail managed the dinner party as best she could under the circumstances, helped by Jennifer who was only too familiar with the situation. When at last the guests had said their goodbyes she kicked off her shoes and looked ruefully at Abigail.

'I hate to say "I told you so", but I'm afraid all this is running very true to form, my pet.'

Abigail sank into a corner of the settee and put her feet up gratefully. 'I know—you don't have to tell me.'

Jennifer helped herself to a brandy, glancing at her daughter. 'Still—if you love him as much as I think you do, maybe you'll have more staying power than I did.' She sat down opposite Abigail and sipped her drink thoughtfully. Suddenly she looked up and asked. 'Have you told him yet that you're pregnant?'

Abigail's eyes flew open as she stared at her mother. 'No—I'm not sure that I am yet. How did you know?'

Jennifer shrugged. 'Call it feminine intuition if you like. I've an idea that Marc's attractive cousin knows too.'

Abigail frowned and shook her head. 'I wish people

wouldn't take such a close interest in me. Why does everyone jump to conclusions so? Just because I was a bit nauseous at the clinic the other day—'

Jennifer reached out to touch her hand. 'Do you *want* to be pregnant, Abby?'

Tears filled her eyes before she could fight them back. 'Yes, very much. Marc wants a son, you see. The family will die out with this generation if there isn't one and—'

'And that *isn't* a good enough reason!' Jennifer looked into her eyes. 'I don't want to pry, darling, but there's something badly wrong between you two. I'm not asking you to tell me what it is, but I *am* asking you to take a break. It's getting you down. Anyone can see that. Why don't you come back with me for a couple of weeks? It would give you time to think things through.'

But Abigail shook her head. 'I can't leave at the moment. There are patients who are relying on me.'

'And who do *you* rely on when it comes to the crunch, Abby?' Jennifer asked. 'Marc is very attractive and you should have everything going for you, yet there's one hell of a barrier between you. I can feel it. I wish you'd let me try to help.'

Abigail tried to smile, swallowing hard at the knot of tears in her throat. 'No one can. I have to work it out for myself,' she said. 'I might take you up on that offer some day soon, but at the moment I'm keeping my fingers crossed that a baby might just tip the scales the right way.'

Jennifer shook her head. 'Oh dear—you *are* in love with him, aren't you? God knows why we women put ourselves through such agony just for mere men!' She yawned and rose to her feet. 'Well, I'm for bed. And I hope you're not thinking of waiting up for that husband of yours.'

'No. I might as well come up too. He could be hours yet.'

As they reached the landing Jennifer turned to her. 'Oh, by the way, it's the glamorous Dr Lesley that Alan Blake is eating his heart out for, isn't it? I've a feeling she loves him too, but it hasn't hit her yet—probably because she's known him so long.'

Abigail shook her head. 'Oh no. You're quite wrong there.'

Jennifer looked at her daughter curiously. 'What makes you so certain?'

'I just know. Lesley's heart is elsewhere and likely to stay there.' She kissed her mother's cheek. 'Good night—sleep well.'

Lying in bed with the lights out, listening to the faint murmur of the sea, Abigail thought about the conversation with Jennifer. She might be wise and perceptive, but she didn't always get it right. Odd that she hadn't seen that it was Marc Lesley wanted, when she had guessed so uncannily at the secret she'd thought was so well hidden. Abigail was glad now that she hadn't had the opportunity of telling Marc this evening. It would be wiser to make quite sure first.

For a long time she lay there, listening for the sound of his car, but at last sleep overtook her. Once she half woke, thinking she heard a footstep on the landing outside—a movement in the dressing-room next door. She smiled and turned over. Soon; soon she would tell him her news, soon the bad dreams would be over and he would be hers again.

CHAPTER TEN

JENNIFER'S short stay came to an end all too soon. Abigail drove her to the airport and hugged her close before waving her off. There was a tight feeling in her throat as they said goodbye. She and her mother had never been so close as they'd become over the past few days, and as she watched the plane take off Abigail wished that she had been able to confide in her more. Jennifer had been through her own troubles and gathered wisdom over the years. Perhaps she could have put things into perspective for her. In the past she had always seemed bitter and cynical about marriage, but this weekend Abigail had glimpsed a softer side to her. She sighed and turned away, glad that tomorrow she would be back, working among her patients.

Since Friday, the evening of the party, she had hardly seen Marc. The patient who had suffered the coronary had been dangerously ill, but was now recovering. He was an old friend of Marc's father and she knew he had been worried about him. Each night when he came in it had been late and he had looked tired, needing only food and sleep. She had tried to talk to him, to let him know that she knew how he felt and sympathised, but it was as though he needed no one.

On Monday morning she woke with a headache and an ominous dull ache low in her back. She got up with a deep sense of depression and disappointment. Dressed in her uniform, she joined Marc at the breakfast table, but almost as soon as she sat down he got up.

'Sorry, but I've got to dash now. I've got a pile of paperwork waiting at the surgery and I promised myself a session with it before surgery starts this morning. Bye.'

She sighed as she watched him disappear through the door. Mrs Morelle brought in her eggs and bacon.

'Better get a good breakfast inside you as you're off to work this morning, Mrs Marcus.' She looked closely at Abigail. 'Are you sure you're fit? You still don't look very well.'

Abigail's lip trembled. She longed to throw herself into the motherly arms and sob—to tell Mrs Morelle that her dreams had been dashed, that the baby she had built such hopes on had never existed after all. But she swallowed back the tears. 'I'm perfectly all right, thank you, Mrs Morelle. I don't think I can eat any breakfast though.'

Mrs Morelle laid a comforting hand on her shoulder. 'There—I expect you'll be missing your mother. What a nice person she is—more like a sister to you than a mother, I dare say.' She poured Abigail a cup of tea. 'There now. Just you have that and some nice toast. Must have something inside you to start the day on.'

Once she had set out on the day's routine, Abigail felt a little better. A couple of aspirins took care of the pain in her back, but she reflected that there was no pill that could cure the ache in her heart. Now there was nothing to tell Marc—and the way things were between them, there never would be. They would live out the year she had agreed to, upholding their sham of a marriage, then she would leave the field clear for Lesley. She thought of Alan. Was Jennifer right about him? Did he really love Lesley? For the first time she felt sorry for him, knowing what he must be going through.

The week dragged wearily by. There were no new

babies born. The work was routine, though for Abigail it was nice to be among her patients again. Marc was busy. There was another practice meeting, this time at DeLisle House. Simon had suggested expanding the surgery building and engaging a resident nurse. There was a lot to discuss. Abigail stood silently on the sidelines, wishing that she could be part of it all, but she said nothing as she listened to the enthusiastic plans being made in the dining-room. She came out into the hall just as Simon and Lesley were leaving, intending to say good night to them. Simon had already gone out to start the car, but Lesley stood with Marc on the porch. As Abigail watched, she saw her stand on tiptoe to kiss his cheek and she drew back, her heart twisting as she saw Marc drop an arm casually round Lesley's shoulders.

'Remember what I told you,' she heard Lesley say quietly. 'Tell her soon. You're a fool to let it go on.'

Abigail slipped into the drawing-room and closed the door, leaning against it, the breath held in her throat. There was no need to ask herself what it was that Marc was being urged to tell her.

It was lunch-time on Friday when the call came. Abigail had just come in and was depositing her hat and case in the hall when Mrs Morelle came through from the kitchen, wiping her floury hands on her apron.

'Oh, I was hoping you'd call in,' she said. 'There was a call for you a little while ago. I was just going to ring the surgery.'

Abigail turned to her. 'Oh—who was it?'

'Mr West. He said he thought his wife had gone into labour.'

Abigail spun round. 'Oh no! She isn't due for another five days. She was booked at the hospital. Has he rung them?'

Mrs Morelle shook her head. 'No. That was part of the message. He said his wife wanted you to see her first. She's afraid it might be a false alarm and she doesn't want to go in only to be sent home again.'

Abigail was already dialling the number. 'There are some emergency obstetric packs in Doctor's study. Will you put one into the car for me, please, just in case? Oh—and the gas and air equipment,' she asked the housekeeper over her shoulder.

The receiver was lifted at the other end and the voice of Sarah, the surgery receptionist, answered.

'Good afternoon. King's Rock Surgery.'

'Oh, Sarah, it's Mrs Marcus. Is Dr Lesley there, please?'

'No, I'm afraid not. She's gone over to Perelle. Nurse Devonish rang her. She has a patient with a threatened miscarriage. Is there anything I can do?'

'If she rings in will you tell her that I'm with Mrs West?' Abigail asked. 'It might be a false alarm, but her husband seems to think she's gone into labour.' She rang off and looked at Mrs Morelle as she picked up her case.

'I daren't stop to eat. It could be tricky. Wish me luck.'

The housekeeper waved her off, trying to reassure her that it was probably nothing. With the disappointments the Wests had had in the past, it wasn't surprising that they should be anxious.

But when Abigail arrived at the house her worst fears were confirmed. Not only was Charlotte in labour, she was in severe pain and almost into her second stage. There was no time to be lost. Abigail examined her and found that the membranes had ruptured. She went downstairs and rang the surgery again, but Lesley still had not returned. She hadn't telephoned in either, and the patient she was with was not on the phone. There was nothing else for it—she must make a decision herself, and make it fast! She opened the door of the living-room where Paul West was pacing the floor. He spun round to search her face anxiously.

'Is she going to be all right?'

Abigail smiled as calmly as she could. 'Don't worry, Mr West. She'll be fine. I wish you'd called me earlier though. She was to have gone into hospital but she's so advanced now that I think I shall have to deliver the baby here.' She looked at him. 'Can you help?'

He nodded eagerly. 'Of course—anything. What do you want me to do?'

'First there is some equipment in the car—gas cylinders and a large sterile pack. You'll see them in the back seat. Then can you help me to raise the bed—blocks of wood, books, anything will do. I'm going to ring the hospital and ask them to have an ambulance standing by in case we need it. Just a precaution,' she added, seeing his worried expression.

In the spotless bathroom she scrubbed up and put on her gown and mask. Paul West carried the equipment upstairs, then helped Abigail to prepare the room for delivery.

Charlotte's second stage was long and agonising. When Abigail had arrived it had been too late for a pethidene injection so that she was already tired, and now she seemed unable to take the gas and air offered. Twice Abigail sent Paul downstairs to ring the surgery, but both times he came back with the news that Lesley still had not returned.

'Shouldn't we get her to the hospital?' he asked anxiously, looking at his wife's exhausted face. 'It's not that I don't have confidence in you, Nurse, just that she was supposed to have this epidural thing—wouldn't that help?'

'I'm afraid it's too late for that now, Mr West,' Abigail told him. She did not add that in Charlotte's present restless state there might be a danger of inadvertantly making a lumbar puncture which would only add to her distress.

It was at eight o'clock, after much pain, with the help and encouragement of her husband and midwife, that Charlotte West gave birth to a baby girl just at the moment when Lesley arrived. For a while all was frenzied activity. Lesley quickly scrubbed up in the bathroom and came back to suture the episiotomy that Abigail had performed just prior to the birth. Paul was despatched downstairs to make tea. Lesley looked at Abigail who was attending to the baby.

'She's very cyanosed, isn't she? Can you clear her airway?'

Abigail was working fast, clearing mucus from the baby's mouth and throat, willing the tiny scrap to take her first breath. If, after all her hard work and pain, Charlotte lost her child she would never forgive herself.

'I understand there's an ambulance on standby,' Lesley said quietly. 'I think perhaps we should send for it now.'

Charlotte was watching anxiously from the bed, aware now that something was wrong. 'What's the matter?' she asked. 'Why doesn't my baby cry? She isn't *dead*, is she?'

'Of course not.' Lesley threw an appealing look at Abigail, who picked up the baby and took her into the bathroom, away from Charlotte's anxious eyes. There she massaged the tiny body and began, very gently, to ventilate her lungs. At last she moved—spluttered and let out her first thin wail. Tears of relief streamed down

Abigail's face as she wrapped the baby up warmly and held her close.

'Thank God—oh, thank God!' she whispered.

Outside the West's house dusk was falling as they stood together by Abigail's car. Lesley laid a hand on her arm.

'You did a fine job. I wonder if they realise just how much they have to thank you for?'

Abigail shook her head. 'Just so long as everything is all right. That's all that matters.' She felt shaken and tearful and she wanted badly to be alone so that she could give way to the emotion that threatened to over-whelm her.

'I'm sorry, but I'm going to have to beg a lift,' Lesley said. 'I was low on petrol when I got back to the surgery. I didn't want to risk running out on the way here so I asked Sarah to give me a lift. I hope you don't mind.'

'Of course not.' Abigail sat in the driving seat and fumbled for her keys. Suddenly it was all too much for her and she laid her head on her folded arms and gave way to the shuddering sobs that shook her whole body. Lesley looked at her in dismay.

'Abby—my dear, what is it?' She slid an arm round the shaking shoulders. 'I know it was touch and go, but you've had tricky cases before, surely?'

Abigail brought her sobs under control and looked at Lesley. There was no point now in keeping anything from her. Soon she would be gone from here. They might never see each other again—what did it matter any more?

'It was just that this time the situation came home to me more,' she said, swallowing hard. 'You see—until a few days ago I thought I might be pregnant myself. The disappointment hit me hard.' Fresh tears began to trickle down her cheeks. 'I—wanted so much to give Marc a son—I believe our marriage depended on it—and now—now it isn't going to happen, ever.'

Lesley sighed and looked at her helplessly for a long moment, then she said decisively, 'I'll drive. You move over into my seat.' She got out of the car and came round, getting into the driving seat and starting the engine without further comment. But as she nosed the car out through the gates and on to the road she glanced at Abigail again. 'I'm taking you to the beach house. I've got my key. It's time we had a talk—there are things you should know, Abby.'

'I know,' Abigail whispered. 'I've known for some time that you and Marc are—'

'No! You only think you know!' Lesley told her abruptly. 'No one knows the real truth but, as Marc's wife, you have a right to. I've been telling him so, but that stubborn pride of his makes him his own worst enemy. He can't get over the fact that you were prepared to believe old Aunt Honoria's accusations.'

The beach was empty and deserted as Lesley unlocked the door of the little stone cottage. They went inside and she switched on the electric fire in the tiny living-room, straightening up to look at Abigail.

'I'll make some coffee in a minute, but first we'll have that talk.'

Abigail sat down and braced herself for what was to come, watching Lesley as she stood at the window, looking out at the sea as though thinking of a way to frame the words. At last she turned to look at Abigail.

'You will have gathered, of course, that Marc and I mean a great deal to one another. When we were children and while we were growing up we were very close. For me, as a small girl, there was no one quite like

Marc. He was my hero—all-wise and all powerful.' She crossed the room to sit down opposite Abigail. 'When I was fourteen my mother fell ill. She grew worse and when she knew that she wouldn't recover she told me the secret that had been troubling her for years. She told me because it was my secret too in a way—mine and Marc's. I was to tell him too after she'd gone—him, but no one else. I've always kept that promise, but now I believe I must break it. I'm sure she would want me to.'

She leaned forward. 'I think you know that Marc's mother deserted him and his father for another man?' Abigail nodded and Lesley went on, 'Marc was very young at the time. His father was shattered when it happened and for a time he and Marc came to stay with my parents. My mother was sympathetic; she'd recently been through a bad time because she was convinced she would never have a child. Stephen turned to her and somehow they found comfort in each other's arms. Later they were both sick with guilt. They ended the affair, vowing not to allow another family disaster. But soon afterwards my mother discovered that she was pregnant—with Stephen's child.'

Abigail stared at her. '*You!*' she whispered. 'It was you—so you and Marc are—'

'Brother and sister.' Lesley nodded. 'He and I have kept it secret all this time. We both love Simon, you see. To me he will always be the father who brought me up so lovingly. When I was born he was so happy. It would break his heart if he ever found out. Stephen never knew that my mother had confessed. That was why he put that clause in his will; he was always terribly afraid we might marry one day. But there is something else you should know, Abby.'

She moved across to where Abigail sat and took her

hand. 'Marc honestly never knew about the marriage clause until the night you arrived here—when you accused him of using you. His father's death was so sudden, you see. Marc had time only for the briefest of visits. He left everything in the hands of Richard Blake, his solicitor, and Richard didn't mention the clause to him because Marc had already confided in him that he hoped to marry very shortly. That night—your wedding night—he went straight to Richard to ask for the truth about it. And that, I promise you, was the first he knew of it.'

Abigail shook her head. 'But why didn't he tell *me* that?'

'Pride. Stupid, stubborn pride! The DeLisles are noted for it. He couldn't come to terms with the fact that you didn't trust him—didn't love him enough.' Lesley smiled ruefully. 'I'm glad I haven't inherited the DeLisle arrogance to that extent!' She pressed Abigail's hand. 'He does love you, Abby. He's been going through hell these past weeks. I've tried everything I could think of to get him to tell you. I even dropped a hint to Alan that you just might be pregnant in the hope that he'd let it slip to Marc. But when none of it worked I decided I couldn't let the two of you go on torturing yourself any longer.'

Abigail sighed, a little numbed by all she had heard. 'What do I do now that I know, though? How do I let Marc know I'm in possession of the facts?'

Lesley stood up. 'Leave that to me. I'll tell him. I'll take all the blame. It'll be worth it to see the pair of you happy again.' She smiled. 'You stay here. Give me an hour. There's food in the kitchen, have something to eat and drink. I'll see that someone comes to collect you soon. It's my guess that someone will be Marc.' She bent to kiss Abigail's forehead. 'You look better already.

You know, it's great to have a sister-in-law, even if I can't let it be known.'

When she had gone, Abigail made herself a hot drink, more to give herself something to do than because she wanted it. Everything fell so neatly into place now. But was it too late? Would Marc ever forgive her for not trusting him? Had she killed the love he had once had for her?

The drink was comforting. It had been a long, exhausting day, both physically and mentally, and as she sat in front of the electric fire she became drowsy. Tangled thoughts tumbled through her mind confusingly; her eyelids grew heavy—too heavy to remain open.

CHAPTER ELEVEN

SHE WOKE with a feeling of disorientation, her limbs stiff and a painful crick in her neck. Looking around her sleepily, she realised that she must have fallen asleep on the settee in the beach house—fallen asleep waiting for Marc to come to her. The electric fire was still on and the room was unbearably hot. Stiffly she rose and switched it off, then crossed the room to draw the curtains. Dawn was just breaking, casting its cool, pearly light over a calm sea. She opened the window and breathed in the fresh, salty air. It cleared the fog in her brain and slowly the events of the past evening came back; Lesley's startling revelation and the new hope it had brought her. But Marc hadn't come to her after all, as Lesley had so confidently predicted. Abigail's spirits sank. Obviously she had been right to wonder if it was all too late. With that fierce pride of his, he couldn't find it in his heart to forgive her in spite of what Lesley had said.

She reached for a chair and sank weakly into it, trying to think of the best course to take. Clearly, there was only one. She must go—leave Guernsey—now, immediately, before another day began. Marc no longer wanted her as his wife. How could she face him again, knowing that?

She looked at her watch. It was a quarter to five. If she began now she could be packed, at the airport and off the island before anyone knew she had gone. Carefully, she began to make her plan.

In the little writing desk she found notepaper and

envelopes. She wrote two notes, one to Marc, the other to Lesley, addressing and sealing them carefully. Then, with a sinking heart, she remembered something—she had no car! True, it was only a short walk to DeLisle House, but the airport was quite a drive away. She had hoped not to involve anyone else, but there seemed no other way. But at least there was one friend who was not a member of the DeLisle family.

She drew the telephone towards her and dialled Alan's number. At the other end of the line it rang—on and on. She was about to give up when there was a click and a drowsy voice answerd, 'Hello—who the hell wants me at this time of the night?'

She sighed with relief. 'Alan, it's me—Abigail. I'm sorry to wake you.'

'Sorry! Do you know what the bloody time is? What's the matter—has World War Three started?'

'Listen, Alan. I want you to do me a favour. I wouldn't ask you if it wasn't desperate, I promise.'

'Desperate? Are you all right, Abby?' He was fully awake now and sounded concerned. 'What is it you want?'

'I want you to take me to the airport.' She swallowed hard. 'Give me about an hour and then wait for me at the gates of DeLisle House.'

He laughed. 'Oh Lord! Is *that* all? You've had a row with old Marc! Look, leaving the island's a bit over the top, isn't it? It'll blow over. Go back to sleep, love. Everything looks bleak at this time of the morning. It'll be—'

'*Alan!*' she interrupted. 'Will you do as I ask—*please*? It isn't just a row—I'm sorry, but I can't go into details. If you can't help me I'll try to get a taxi—if I can raise one at this hour.'

He sighed gustily. 'All right, all right. You're right about the taxis—they've got more sense than me. They don't answer the phone at non-existent hours like this. The gates of DeLisle House in about an hour, you said—okay, I'll be there, God help me!'

With a sigh of relief she hung up, gathered her things together and carefully locked the cottage.

DeLisle House was silent as she let herself in. Abigail climbed the stairs, grateful for the thick carpet that muffled her footsteps. In her room she set about packing as quickly as she could; there was no time to be lost. Stripping off her crumpled uniform, she changed into a sensible suit for travelling, then she took the envelope addressed to Marc from her handbag and propped it up on the dressing-table, anchoring it with the DeLisle ruby ring in its velvet box.

When she had finished she stood for a long moment, looking around her. This room had seen some bitter quarrels and a lot of misery, but it had also seen the one night of blissful happiness that she and Marc had shared. Tears well up in her eyes as she recalled that night. He had loved her then, there could be no denying it. The memory filled her with a desperate, aching longing and she turned her back abruptly on the four-poster bed, unable to bear the thought that she would never share it with him again. She stared uncertainly at the door of the dressing-room, toying with the thought of opening it to take one last look at the man sleeping on the other side, but she turned away before she could give in to the temptation. Marc was a light sleeper, like most doctors. She dared not take the risk.

It was ten to six when she left DeLisle House for the last time and set off down the drive. Alan was waiting near the gates with his car, and when he saw her he got out and opened the boot, taking the case from her hand and swinging it inside. He gave her a rueful grin.

'I hope you know that you're putting me in a rotten position,' he admonished. 'Marc'll probably never speak to me again when he knows I've aided and abetted you in this.'

She climbed unsmilingly into the car and fastened her seat-belt. 'On the contrary, you're doing him a favour,' she told him grimly. He turned in his seat to look at her.

'Tell me to mind my own business if you like—but you're not just doing this to teach Marc a lesson, are you?'

She shook her head. 'I'm not given to flamboyant gestures, Alan. No. It's more final than that, I'm afraid.'

He sighed as he started the engine. 'Oh dear—want to talk about it?'

'Not that I don't want to—I can't.' She turned her head away so that he wouldn't see her brimming eyes. 'Just for the record though, Alan, I want you to know that it's entirely *my* fault. Our marriage is over and it's because of me—so don't ever let anyone tell you any different.'

He gave her a sympathetic little half grin. 'Go on— have a good cry if you want to. Tissues in the glove compartment.'

She lifted her chin. 'I'm all right, thanks.'

'Have you any idea where you're going—or on what flight?' he asked.

She shrugged. 'All I could think of was getting away as quickly as I could.'

'I take it it'll be London. Actually, while I was waiting I took the liberty of ringing to enquire. There's a flight to

Heathrow at eight forty-five. Should be just right.'

She reached out to touch his arm. 'Oh, Alan—that was thoughtful. You're a real friend.'

He sighed. 'To tell you the truth, I've felt sort of responsible for you ever since the day I saved your life. It was the only noble thing I've ever done, you see—my one unselfish deed, shining away like a diamond in a pigsty. And now the only living evidence of it is going away!'

She laughed softly. 'Alan, I think you're a bit of a phoney—a much nicer person than you let anyone believe.'

He looked at her with raised eyebrows. 'Well! There's a backhanded compliment if ever I heard one!'

'I mean it,' she told him. 'What's more, I think I've guessed your secret. It's Lesley—isn't it?'

He shrugged. 'I had hoped it didn't show.' He glanced at her. 'Now that you're leaving Marc, I may as well tell you. I think Lesley has always had a secret thing for him. Maybe it's returned . . . I don't know, but I've always felt he was my greatest rival.'

Abigail looked at him for a long moment. 'Alan, don't ask me to explain, but I happen to know without any doubt that you're wrong. I'm sure you could win Lesley if you'd only let her see you as you really are. Drop that facade of brashness and let her know how deep your feelings really go. I wouldn't mind betting it'd work like a charm.' She sighed. 'I only wish my problem could be solved as easily.'

At the airport he waited with her until the flight was called, even though she urged him to leave. From time to time he looked anxiously at her.

'I can't help feeling that I shouldn't be letting you go like this,' he said with genuine concern. 'Letting you go off like this is going to put me in a lot of people's bad books.'

'Then don't tell them,' she told him firmly. 'I certainly shan't. No one need ever know.'

As the flight was called she reached up to kiss his cheek. 'Thanks, Alan. I appreciate all you've done for me. And remember what I said about Lesley. Good luck!'

He hugged her close for a moment, then watched as she disappeared into the crowd.

Once on the plane the realisation of what she had done hit her—the finality of it. The aircraft taxied out to the runway, then began its take-off with a roar of engines. As it lifted into the air she saw again the glitter and sparkle, the emerald greenness of the beautiful island that had been her home so briefly, and the tears filled her eyes as she remembered seeing it for the first time on her wedding day, with Marc beside her, pointing out the landmarks with such pride. Perhaps she would never see it again, but the memory would remain in her heart for ever. She turned her head so that the elderly lady sitting beside her would not see her distress. Slowly the plane climbed into the sky, higher and higher until the little island was lost to view and all she could see was billowing clouds.

'Have a peppermint, dear?'

The gentle voice made her jump and she turned to see the sweet-faced old lady holding out a packet to her.

'I know how you feel,' she said. 'I love this place too. Been coming here for my holidays for the last twenty years. My husband and I always promised ourselves we'd make our home here when we retired. He was a Guernsey man, you see. But he died last year and somehow it wouldn't feel right without him.'

Abigail took one of the sweets offered and smiled sympathetically. 'I know how you must feel,' she said sincerely.

She telephoned Jennifer's office from the airport. A secretary put her through. Jennifer's voice was crisp and cool.

'Jennifer Brent here. Can I help you?'

'Hello, it's me—Abby.'

There was a shocked pause, then, 'Darling! Where are you?'

'Here, in London. At least, at the airport. I thought I'd take you up on that offer.'

'Offer? What offer? Abby—are you all right? You sound odd.'

Abigail forced a laugh. 'I'm fine. Surely you haven't forgotten urging me to take a break.'

'No—no, of course I haven't, but—'

'Well, here I am. Is there any way I can get into the flat?'

'The caretaker has a pass key. I'll ring him. And I'll come home in my lunch-break.'

'No! Please don't bother. Just so long as I can get in I'll be fine. See you later. I mustn't stop you from working. Bye.' And before Jennifer could ask any more probing questions, she rang off. She needed time to think out what she was going to say, though she knew that in the end she would have to come clean.

At Jennifer's flat the caretaker let her in. Abigail unpacked and made up one of the beds in the guest room for herself. It was only then that she realised how tired she was. She couldn't have had more than a couple of hours' sleep last night—and that had been slumped on the settee at the beach house with her clothes on.

Stripping off her skirt and jacket, she crept under the duvet and in five minutes she had fallen into a deep, exhausted sleep.

She awoke to someone shaking her shoulder and opened her eyes to look sleepily into Jennifer's anxious face.

'Darling! Are you all right? I thought you'd never wake! You haven't taken anything, have you?'

Abigail pulled herself into a sitting position. 'No—I was so tired—up most of last night.'

Jennifer sat on the edge of the other bed. 'I can imagine! I came home as soon as I saw the paper. I didn't know about it until Sandra, my secretary showed me the headlines in the later editions. It must have been terrible. Poor Marc! But I don't understand why you're here and not with him.'

Abigail was wide awake now. She stared at her mother, a feeling of apprehension beginning to gnaw at her stomach. 'What are you talking about? What must have been terrible? What has happened to Marc?' She began to get out of bed, but Jennifer put out a hand to stop her, her face concerned.

'Abby—you mean you don't know?'

'Don't know *what*?' Abigail shouted. 'For heaven's sake stop talking in riddles and tell me what's happened to my husband!' She was on her feet now and facing her mother, her heart beating fast and her knees like jelly.

Jennifer put out her hands to steady her. 'Take it easy. There was a fire at the hospital at King's Rock. No one seems to know how it started. They think it must have been an electrical fault—'

'Never mind all that. What about Marc?' Abigail grasped her mother's shoulders. 'What was he doing there—what happened to him? *Tell me!*'

Jennifer pressed her back on to the bed. Calm down, Abby. It's all right. It says in the paper that Marc received only superficial burns. Apparently he was very brave—rushing in without any thought for his own safety and bringing out several of the immobile patients—especially babies. It was in the maternity unit, you see. I'm only glad I *didn't* see the paper before you rang! I'd have been out of my mind with worry!'

But Abigail wasn't listening. In her mind the events of the past hours were clicking into place. All the time she had been silently packing at DeLisle House Marc had been at the hospital—not asleep in the dressing room at all! While she had slept at the beach house, the fire had been burning without her knowledge. While she was flying out of the island Marc had been hurt—needing her, possibly quite unaware of the conversation she and Lesley had had. By now he had probably gone home—and found her note! Her hand flew to her mouth.

'Oh God! What have I done?' She sank on to the bed and began to sob. All the pent-up emotion of the past twenty-four hours, plus the shock of what she had just learned, catching up with her. Jennifer sat down beside her and slid an arm round her shoulders, drawing her close.

'Don't cry like that, darling,' she whispered. 'I think you have a little explaining to do yourself now, don't you?'

Slowly, Abigail poured it all out; admitting her initial doubts about the whirlwind love affair and hasty marriage; her disillusionment when she thought that Marc had married her simply in order to benefit from his father's will; her shattered hopes for a baby to heal the rift—and finally last night's misunderstanding.

'All I could think of was myself,' she moaned. 'While Marc was risking his life! What will he think of me?'

But Jennifer was busy fishing the suitcase out from under the divan where Abigail had kicked it, taking the clothes from the wardrobe and folding them. 'I think you know what you must do,' she said. 'Look, you carry on with this packing while I go and ring the airport—find out whether there's a flight tonight.'

But she had scarcely reached the bedroom door when the telephone rang. They looked at each other, then Abigail said, 'I'll go. They'll have guessed I'm here. There may be some news.'

The voice at the other end was Alan's. 'Thought I'd better put you in the picture in case you were worried,' he said. 'You've heard the news, I expect?'

'Yes—just now.' Her mouth was dry and her voice almost inaudible. 'Oh, Alan—if only I'd waited! How is Marc? Do you know?'

'He's all right—just superficial burns to his hands. I don't know if you've seen the papers but he was quite a hero, saved several lives. The thing is though—he thought *you* were in there. Some mix-up over a baby that should have been born there last night and wasn't after all. Lesley told me. She was pretty mad with me for letting you go. That's why I'm ringing.'

'As long as he's all right. Thank God—oh, thank God!' Abigail bit her lip. Mrs Morelle would have given Marc the message about the West baby; of course, he would think she was at the hospital! 'Alan—the note,' she said, holding her breath. 'Do you know if he opened the note I left him?'

'I don't know about Marc, but it was after Lesley read hers that she rang me!'

'I'm coming right back,' she told him. 'I'll be leaving as soon as I can get a flight.'

'Look—hold on, Abby. Marc's not here. That's what I've been trying to tell you. Lesley said he rang her father and asked him to hold the fort. He didn't say where he was going—just that he'd be back soon.'

As she replaced the receiver Abigail looked at her mother. 'Did you hear all that?' Jennifer nodded helplessly and she sank on to a chair. 'What a mess! Oh, Jennifer, what shall I do?'

'Well, at least you know that Marc's all right.' Jennifer smiled reassuringly. 'Stay here for tonight. You're exhausted anyway. Tomorrow you can ring and find out whether they've heard any more.' She looked at Abigail's white face. 'You look all in, darling. Why don't you have a hot bath and change? I don't suppose you've eaten either?'

Abigail shook her head. 'Not since this morning—on the plane.'

'I thought as much. Look, there's a nice little restaurant round the corner that does lovely meals to take away. I'll go and get one while you have a bath. Everything will look better when you've eaten.' She began to put on her coat, calling over her shoulder, 'Put in plenty of that Chanel bath essence. I got it in New York and it's sheer heaven!'

Abigail did as she was told. In the warm, scented water she began to relax and unwind, letting all that Alan had told her sink in. At least Marc was safe. If anything had happened to him while he was trying to save her she would never have forgiven herself.

She got out of the bath and dried herself, then slipped on a nightdress and dressing-gown. Tomorrow she must go back and sort the whole mess out. However much she wanted to, there was nothing she could do tonight. She was just coming out of the bathroom when the front doorbell rang. She turned towards the hall. Jennifer must have forgotten her key in her hurry to buy the food!

'A good job I was out of the bath,' she said as she opened the door. 'A moment sooner and you—' Her words tailed off as she stood staring up at the man outside. Roughly, he pushed past her into the flat, his brows drawn together angrily.

'So *this* is where you are! Do you realise I've been ringing all round the country, trying to find out where you'd gone?'

She closed the door and stood facing him, lost for words. If he had really gone into that blazing hospital, risking his life because he thought she was in danger, he had a strange way of showing it. She began to turn away but he caught at her wrist.

'Don't walk away from me! I want an explanation. What does all this mean? Why did you leave?' He fished in an inside pocket and brought out the note she had left him. 'And just what is this all about?'

She looked up at him, her lip trembling. 'Last night Lesley told me the secret about her birth—the relationship between you.' She bit her lip. 'She told me other things too—about your father's will. Afterwards she left me at the beach house while she went to talk to you. I waited for you to come. I must have fallen asleep eventually and when I woke I thought . . . The answer seemed obvious—you hadn't come because you didn't want me any more. I—'

He clutched her shoulders. 'You took off—just like that! Without waiting to find out what had happened?'

'I didn't know about the fire—how could I?' she protested. 'It was very early. All I could think of was

getting away before I could embarrass you any further.'
Tears welled up in her eyes. 'When I heard about the fire
and about what you did, I felt terrible. I was going to
come straight back.'

'And what then?' he demanded. 'What would you
have done *then*?' His fingers gripped her shoulders hard
and painfully as he held her fast, looking down into her
eyes angrily. 'You'd have asked for your divorce in a
civilised way, I suppose, and that would have made the
whole thing correct!'

She swallowed hard at the knot of tears in her throat.
'What do you *want*, Marc?' she whispered huskily.
'What do you want me to do? It's something you've
never actually told me, so how can I know?'

For a long moment he stared at her, his eyes enigmatic, then he dropped his hands to his sides and walked
away, his back towards her.

'I want you, Abby,' he said at last. 'I want you to come
back to King's Rock with me and be my wife.' He turned
to look at her. The anger had gone now from his eyes and
in them she saw her own pain reflected. 'I mean really
my wife,' he went on. 'Not the miserable sham we've
been living since we were married. That's what I want—
what I've always wanted. A wife who believed and
trusted me—loved me as I loved her.'

She took a step towards him, the ache in her heart
almost unbearable. 'I do love you, Marc. I've never
stopped loving you,' she whispered. 'That's what made it
so hard. If only you'd told me at the beginning—' She
stopped, shaking her head and she tried to find the
words. 'We'd known each other for such a short time. I
knew so very little about you.'

He held out his arms and she went into them, clinging
to him as the tears coursed down her cheeks. 'You can

never know how much I wanted to believe you,' she told him. 'But you offered no explanation to any of my fears—no answers.'

He stopped her words with a kiss, then pressed her head into the hollow of his shoulder, stroking her hair. 'I know. I've been an arrogant boor. I should have told you the things you had a right to know months ago.' He tipped her chin up and searched her eyes. 'Darling, listen—we need time to ourselves. To make up for what we've lost—to get to know each other all over again. You never had a honeymoon, Abigail. What would you say to a few days right away from everyone and everything we know—say in Paris?'

She looked at him with shining eyes. 'Oh, Marc—*could* we?'

'Well really! I turn my back for a few minutes and come back to find two people arranging a honeymoon in my living-room!'

They turned in surprise to see Jennifer standing in the doorway. Neither of them had heard her come in. Her eyes twinkled as she added, 'In case anyone is interested I've brought a take-away meal—and I've just remembered something. I have to go out this evening—dinner with the managing director of an advertising agency we deal with. I may be rather late back, but I don't suppose you'll mind that. Will you excuse me if I go and change now?'

As she turned, Abigail took a step towards her, a protest on her lips, but Marc put out his hand to draw her back.

'Let her go. Jennifer knows what she's doing.' His eyes twinkled as he looked at her. 'We'd better eat that food she's brought before it gets cold. It would look churlish not to.' He kissed the tip of her nose. 'Will you lay the table while I dish up?' As she turned he pulled her to him again. 'But not yet—not for a moment. First I want to hold you again, just to make sure I'm not dreaming. Later I'll ring the airport and see if they have a flight to Paris in the morning, but for me that honeymoon starts here and now!'

He held her close, as though he would never let her go, and her heart was full. There was so much she wanted to tell him, so much to say, but as his lips found hers she knew that there were other, sweeter ways with which to tell him than with words.

New from Violet Winspear, one of Mills and Boon's best-selling authors, a longer romance of mystery, intrigue, suspense and love. Almost twice the length of a standard romance for just £1.95. Published on the 14th of June.

The Rose of Romance

Mills & Boon

4 Doctor Nurse Romances
FREE

Coping with the daily tragedies and ordeals of a busy hospital, and sharing the satisfaction of a difficult job well done, people find themselves unexpectedly drawn together. Mills & Boon Doctor Nurse Romances capture perfectly the excitement, the intrigue and the emotions of modern medicine, that so often lead to overwhelming and blissful love. By becoming a regular reader of Mills & Boon Doctor Nurse Romances you can enjoy SIX superb new titles every two months plus a whole range of special benefits: your very own personal membership card, a free newsletter packed with recipes, competitions, bargain book offers, plus big cash savings.

AND an Introductory FREE GIFT for YOU.
Turn over the page for details.

**Fill in and send this coupon back today
and we'll send you
4 Introductory
Doctor Nurse Romances yours to keep**
FREE
At the same time we will reserve a
subscription to Mills & Boon
Doctor Nurse Romances for you. Every
two months you will receive the latest
6 new titles, delivered direct to your door.
You don't pay extra for delivery. Postage and
packing is always completely Free.
There is no obligation or commitment –
you receive books only for
as long as you want to.

**It's easy! Fill in the coupon below and return it to
MILLS & BOON READER SERVICE, FREEPOST, P.O. BOX 236,
CROYDON, SURREY CR9 9EL.**

**Please note: READERS IN SOUTH AFRICA write to
Mills & Boon Ltd., Postbag X3010,
Randburg 2125, S. Africa.**

FREE BOOKS CERTIFICATE
To: Mills & Boon Reader Service, FREEPOST, P.O. Box 236,
Croydon, Surrey CR9 9EL.

Please send me, free and without obligation, four Dr. Nurse Romances, and reserve a Reader
Service Subscription for me. If I decide to subscribe I shall receive, following my free parcel of
books, six new Dr. Nurse Romances every two months for £6.00*, post and packing free. If I
decide not to subscribe, I shall write to you within 10 days. The free books are mine to keep in
any case. I understand that I may cancel my subscription at any time simply by writing to you. I
am over 18 years of age.
Please write in BLOCK CAPITALS.

Name _____

Address _____

_____

_____

_____ Postcode _____

SEND NO MONEY — TAKE NO RISKS

Remember, postcodes speed delivery. Offer applies in UK only and a not valid to present subscribers. Mills &
Boon reserve the right to exercise discretion in granting membership. If price changes are
8DN necessary you will be notified. Offer expires 31st December 1985.
* Subject to possible V.A.T.

EP15